WILL BROWN

Copyright ©2021 by William Brown

All rights reserved. Printed in the United States of America. No part of this book may be reproduced in any manner whatsoever without written permission except in the case of brief quotations embodied in critical articles and review.

Published by Literati Publishing
www.literatipublishing.website

Cover design by University of Moguls Publishing and Design
www.universityofmoguls.com

ISBN-13: 9798710751466

For speaking engagements and bulk book orders:
William Brown
literatibooks11@yahoo.com

Website:
www.literatipublishing.website

Instagram:
@literati_publishing

Twitter:
@literatipublishing

*Dedicated to my mother and father.
Without you, there would be no me.*

ACKNOWLEDGEMENTS

First and foremost, I would like to thank God almighty for everything. I would like to thank both my mom and dad, my sister, and everyone who has believed in me from the very beginning.

This book is a work of fiction.

CHAPTER 1

"Fuck that tight motherfucka," Brenda said to her close friend and get high partner, Reka, about her own son. "... that nigga want to sit up in my house all day making money, and then got the nerve to get an attitude when I ask for some love."

"Calm down Brenda," Reka said. "You know Craig think he Ron O'Neil or somebody. Let me go talk to him and see if I can get us something. He might be a little more in the giving mood for me."

"Yeah, you go talk to him. You know he sweet on you," Brenda said, encouraging Reka to seduce her son in exchange for crack.

The aforementioned exchange between Reka and Brenda's son Craig had been taking place ever since Craig was fifteen with Brenda's blessing. As Reka headed off towards Craig's bedroom with hopes of procuring the drug, she made a quick pit stop in the bathroom to wash just in case he wanted more than just some head.

Reka had been selling her body for crack ever since the first day she had started smoking it. To her, it was the easiest way to obtain the highly-addictive narcotic. Most of the men who had it—whether it be user or dealer—were willing to part with some of it for either a ride on her wide hips, or a suckling from her full lips. Even with all the years of drug abuse and life on the streets, Reka was still pretty and had the type of curves and eyes that drove men wild. Her high-yellow skin and light brown eyes exuded sex appeal.

As she prepared to knock on Craig's door, Reka tugged down at the dingy tank top she wore, exposing her deep cleavage. She then gave her nipples a quick rub, causing them to tense up and push through her shirt since there was no bra to contain them.

Reka knocked three times on Craig's door, and then waited for him to answer.

"Yeah?" A heavy voice answered from the other side of the door.

Reka twisted the knob to open the door. Entering the room, she was confronted by rap music and weed smoke. As she walked thru, Craig looked up to see who it was, and then quickly shook his head and said one word, "No."

Reka continued on as if she did not hear him and took a seat on the couch in the room next to Craig's little brother, Kevin, who everybody called Kev for short. Kev was thirteen years old and small and skinny.

"Hey little man," Reka greeted him. She leaned in to kiss Kev on the cheek, but came up empty as Kev deftly dodged her lips.

"Don't be like that to your auntie," she said as she rustled the hair on his head. Kev had never really liked Reka because he knew she was getting high with his mother. Even if he didn't fully understand what they were doing, he did, however, always see the end results which left no doubt in his mind that it was bad. His brother Craig didn't put any cut on it when he had explained to Kev what was going on.

"Mom and Reka are crackheads," he had told his little bro. "All they want to do is get high... they don't give a fuck about nothing or nobody, not even us. All they care about is this." He pulled out a crack rock and showed it to his little brother. "This is crack," he had said. "... crack gets you money and money gets you anything... so crack can get you anything."

Kev decided then that one day he would sell crack too, so that he could get anything he wanted.

Even though Kev attended school daily, Craig made it his business to give Kev a different, more real type of schooling. After the death of their middle brother, Clyde—who had drowned while Brenda was getting high—Craig vowed to raise Kev and prepare him for anything. He had already taught him the ins and outs of the dope game along with many other jewels about street life.

"What's up Reka?" Craig asked saving Kev from the much unwanted attention.

"Well... I need to talk to you."

"You got some money?" He asked.

"No, but I was hoping that we could work something out."

As she finished her sentence, Reka leaned forward, exposing the top of her breasts through the opening of her shirt. She then licked her lips in a suggestive manner.

Craig's manhood started awakening uncontrollably as he watched the seductive harlot.

"Kev, take this and run up to the store and buy some snacks," Craig said, extending a ten-dollar bill to his brother. Kev took the money and left the room, leaving Reka alone with Craig.

As soon as the door closed, Reka positioned herself down on her knees between Craig's legs and began removing her top. Resting her breasts on his lap, she took him in her mouth. Moaning and mumbling as she worked on him, Craig pushed her head down on his lap and held it there until the job was done.

When she was finished, Craig stood up with a smile on his face while he zipped and buttoned his pants back up. "So, what do I owe you?"

After wiping her mouth Reka slipped her tank top back over her head. "Just something for me and your mom to wake up off of."

"Shit y'all ain't been asleep all week." Craig started laughing. He reached into his pants pocket and pulled out a sandwich bag that contained about fifty rocks in it. He removed one and then placed it in Reka's hand.

"Is that it?" She asked with obvious disappointment. "C'mon Craig, give auntie some fucking with, I told you I was going to share it with Brenda."

"Well that's on you, 'cause I ain't giving her shit unless she got some money, 'cause she sure as hell ain't sucking me for one."

Reka was mad. She knew Brenda and her could split the rock and still get high, but she wanted her own so she could save some for when she started to come down. Seeing that Craig was resolute in his decision, she figured the only way to get another piece was to do what she did best; so she stood up and lowered her pants and panties and then turned around to look back at Craig.

"Come here," she said as she bent over on the bed at the waist.

"Nah I'm good. Go ahead and pull your pants back up."

Reka ignored him, and instead inserted her finger into her pussy and started fingering herself at a rapid pace. Craig could only stare as she went to work on herself. He felt his manhood harden again and unconsciously reached his hand down to squeeze on it.

"Fuck it," he said then freed himself from his pants once again.

Reka welcomed the pounding with the experience of a lifelong pro.

Just when Craig was getting into her good, the door opened, and little Kev walked in carrying a bag of goodies.

He stood there silent watching for a second then cleared his throat. "Um... Umm..." He said, not sure of what to do.

Craig and Reka finally took notice of Kev's arrival in the room, but neither one of them thought about stopping. "Come back in a few minutes, Kev," Craig said in a strained voice without breaking rhythm.

Kev did as he was told and left the room, leaving the two adults alone to finish their activities. After ten minutes had passed, he returned to the room only to find both Reka and his brother gone. He heard the shower running in the bathroom next to the room he was in and guessed that it was Craig. His assumption was proved correct once his big brother reentered the room with a towel wrapped around his waist.

"You saw what me and Reka was doing?" Craig asked as he was getting dressed.

Kev nodded his head.

"Do you know what it's called?"

Kev nodded once again. "Sex."

"That's right sex. Fucking. Doin' it. It's all the same. What men call it is getting some pussy. Next to money, pussy is the best thing on Earth."

Kev was attentively listening; taking note he decided that he would get him some pussy too, and the sooner the better.

Craig finished getting dressed then brushed his hair and doused himself in cologne. He was tall and dark-skinned with strong prominent facial features and broad shoulders on a slim frame. He was far from model beauty, but his demeanor and confidence made him attractive. Once he had finished getting himself together, he gave himself a once-over in the mirror, then walked over to the corner of the room and removed the baseboard off the wall revealing a hole. Kev watched as Craig reached his hand in the hole and pulled out a wad of cash and the same baggie full of rocks he'd had on him earlier.

"See Kev," Craig started as he began tucking away his belongings. "You can't ever leave anything out when you live with crackheads. You always got to put up. Shit ain't even safe in your pants pocket while you in the shower."

Kev watched as his brother put the baseboard back in place and took note of that lesson too.

They left the house and climbed in Craig's suburban and then cruised the west side streets of Akron, Ohio.

Craig's Suburban was ten years old but had low miles, a custom paint job, big rims, and a deafening sound system on which he kept trap rap music playing.

After filling up at a gas station on Copley road where the Suburban's gas tank tried to break Craig's pockets, they went to a store on V. Odom that had used to be a record shop back when Craig was a kid. The sales attendant was a nice-looking young lady with a radiant smile and curvy figure.

After one look at Kev, she asked if he liked a young rapper who had a hit record that was hot. Kev nodded his head vigorously. Kev knew exactly who she was talking about and loved the song. All the boys and girls at his school liked the song and participated in the dance every time they heard it; something about a beat box was the only words Kev actually understood though.

"You ought to download this song for your brother," the salesgirl said, turning her attention to Craig who was looking at some shirts on a rack.

"Who?" Craig asked having never heard of the young rapper before.

"You know... the dance," the girl said while demonstrating the dance moves bringing a smile to both his and Kev's face. Craig thought the moves resembled the "walk like an Egyptian" dance from back in the day, only with more flare.

"Oh yeah!" Craig said, now recognizing the song. "You want that, lil bro?"

Kev nonchalantly nodded his head, trying to be cool even though he was thrilled inside. Craig promised he'd download the song then asked about some skin care products that were on display. The salesgirl told him that it was a local product and that it worked really well.

"Oh, that's the face soap Lucky been advertising on IG," Craig said

"Yep, that's him, you know him?"

Craig nodded his head; he had gone to high school with Lucky and always knew he'd be an entrepreneur. Craig found it cool that he could now buy commercial products from his old classmates.

After purchasing a bar of soap along with the face scrub, they left the store and got back in the truck to continue their day. Kev reminded Craig about downloading the song, then they rode down Copley Road playing it loud enough to wake the dead. Kev loved Craig more than words could explain. He was literally his everything. Not only did he provide him with his food, shelter, and clothing, making sure he stayed fresh; but he did all the little extra things too, like agreeing to let him blast the song through the speakers even though he had a rule that only trap music would ever be played in his ride.

They stopped at a stop light on the corner of Copley and Packard and saw three girls that looked to be around Craig's age standing next to a car in the parking lot of a store everyone in the hood called "O.P." When the girls heard the music, they each looked toward the suburban and started doing the dance moves.

"Boy, you might know something," Craig said to Kev and then gave the trio of young ladies a head nod.

The girls waved and smiled back flirtatiously, enticing Craig to pull into the parking lot. Kev watched how Craig picked the prettiest one by beckoning her to the truck and asking her for her name and phone number, then feeding her an endless stream of compliments which she took graciously.

When his cell rang interrupting their conversation, Craig took the call and quickly ended it by telling whoever it was on the other end that he'd be there in ten minutes. He told the young lady that he had to go because money had called, which she agreed he should go tend to, but made him promise to call her before he left; which he did with true intentions to do so. Once they were back on the road, Craig turned the music down and turned to Kev.

"You see how them hoes go to sweating a nigga?"

Kev nodded.

"Now if I was walking with dirty clothes and busted shoes, you think they would have even given me the time of day?"

"Not a chance," Kev answered, shaking his head.

"That's right. They might choose you for your looks, popularity, or intelligence when you're young, but once you're grown it's all about the dough. It's the money they want when you get older. What kind of car you drive, what kind of jewelry you wear, and most importantly, what you're willing to spend on them."

"Are all women like that?" Kev asked.

"All of 'em," Craig answered flatly. "You see how quick she told me to go and get that money?" Kev nodded.

"Just remember this, lil bro, you'll always lose money while chasing a bitch, but you'll never lose a bitch while chasing money."

Craig let that last statement hang in the air for a moment before using the remote to his car stereo to unmute the music which was now playing Craig's playlist. Kev knew his brother was now in "hustle mode." Whenever he listened to Lil Baby, Yo Gotti, or Moneybagg, Kev knew Craig thought he was Cleveland Ken or somebody. They hadn't made it halfway through the first song when Craig hit mute on the stereo.

"Don't look back Kev," He said in a hushed tone.

Kev knew by the command along with the apprehension in it that the cops were behind them.

"Take this and put it inside your briefs," Craig said passing Kev his bag of rocks.

Kev put the drugs inside his briefs with no hesitation and with as little movement as possible just as the flashing blue lights started reflecting off of everything around them.

Craig pulled the Suburban over to the side of the road, put it in park and then turned off the engine. He had been through this routine plenty of times before and already knew the drill. By the time the officer approached his car door, he was already holding his driver's license and insurance in his hand with both hands placed on the steering wheel in clear view.

"Get out of the car," the white officer said while tugging on the locked door handle.

In any other circumstance, this would have been an illegal action, but since this was a "weed and seed" neighborhood, it gave the police free reign to just about do as they pleased with little to no probable cause. Craig knew this, so he reluctantly unlocked the door. The police officer, who was sworn to protect and serve, yanked the door open and forcefully removed Craig from the vehicle. Craig allowed the cop to be rough with him as he was being pulled out of the truck but once the overzealous officer tried to slam him onto the ground, Craig started to resist, leading to a struggle.

The ensuing struggle didn't last long. Instead of Craig being slammed to the ground, he easily overpowered and outwrestled the officer, slamming him to the ground onto the crown of his head causing his scalp to split at the hairline. As soon as Craig saw the blood running down the officer's face, he knew he had made a big mistake. As the officer was reaching for his gun, Craig realized how dire the consequences of his mistake actually were and turned to run away but to no avail.

POW! POW! POW! The shots rang out from the officer's gun, all finding their designated target.

Craig's body slammed onto the ground as red blood splattered the pavement.

As Craig lay in an expanding red puddle of his own blood trying to breathe with holes in his lungs, he looked up and towards the open door of the Suburban and saw Kev kneeling over the driver's seat with his mouth agape and his eyes bulging. Kev watched as his older brother's body twitched trying to hang on to life.

"Damn," Craig thought "You're on your own now, lil man," he whispered as his last breath slipped out and he lay still with his eyes open staring at Kev.

CHAPTER 2

The police took Kev to the precinct and tried to be extra nice to him as if he hadn't just witnessed one of their own gun down his brother. They couldn't question him about what he'd witnessed because he was a minor, so instead they just offered him their shallow condolences and tried to give him food and drink. Kev wanted no part of anything they had to offer. After shedding those initial tears at the scene of the shooting, he took on a quiet calm demeanor that made him resemble a shell of a real human. He was in shock. He still couldn't believe what had just happened. He kept telling himself that he was going to be okay but in reality, he was terrified because he knew things were anything but. His head hurt and his chest felt as if a hole was burrowed deep through it and his entire body felt weak making him sleepy. The pain was unbearable.

After waiting for almost an hour, a Black woman in a gray business suit entered the room and took a seat at the table adjacent to him

"Hello Kevin, my name is Mrs. Brown and I'm from the Children's Service Board. Do you know how we can reach your mother? You know, like a phone number or address?" she said.

Kev looked at the pretty Black woman and felt a little less defensive. "Our address is 950 Greenwood. We don't got no phone though," he said, sounding morose.

Mrs. Brown wrote the address down in a pocket notebook then looked back up at Kev. "You want to tell me what happened?"

A solid tear escaped from Kev's right eye and coasted down his cheek as he reflected on the incident. He shook his head no to her question.

"I understand if you don't want to talk about it. It was a very unfortunate, tragic incident. Just know that the police are going to need your help in order to get to the bottom of this and see what happened out there."

His help, Kev thought. He would never help the police with anything. He wouldn't even give them directions if they asked. Craig had told him a while back to never cooperate or put the police in your business in any way, because they'd only make things worse and Kev believed he was right.

"Well, we're going to send someone to your house so someone can come and get you. Who is your legal guardian? Your mother?"

"No, it was my brother."

"I see. Well is there anyone else who will look after you?"

"Yeah, my mom lives in the house with us," Kev answered.

"That's great," she responded, contrary to Kev's belief. "We'll go there and tell her what's happened, then release you to her after she fills out some paperwork, okay?"

Kev nodded in affirmation.

Mrs. Brown then rose to her feet and headed towards the door but stopped short before exiting and looked back at Kev.

"Don't worry Kev, everything is going to be all right."

Kev dropped his head, breaking their eye contact. He was not so sure about that assessment, and she secretly agreed. She had been doing this job for over ten years and had seen this scenario plenty of times before. She had a feeling that this story would not have a happy ending.

Kev watched as she turned and walked out the door, leaving him alone in the room. He sat reminiscing on all the good times he had shared with Craig for what felt like hours before the door opened again and Mrs. Brown crossed its threshold, alone. One look at her face let Kev know that something was wrong. She walked to the table without saying a word and moved the chair she had sat on earlier from across the table to right next to Kev.

"I'm going to be straight up with you Kevin. Your mom isn't coming."

The blow hurt just as much as watching Craig get killed. Kev knew that his mom was a crackhead, and that she was bad off, but he never would have thought in a million years that she didn't want him or would just leave him on his own.

"I need you to think hard now, Kevin... is there anyone else who might be willing to come and get you? Auntie, uncle, cousin? Family friend? Anybody?"

Kev took a moment to think then slowly shook his head no. There was no one. Mrs. Brown exhaled deeply feeling her own share of hurt.

"Kevin, if there is no one who's willing to look after you, then you will have to come with me until I find you a home."

Kev's spirits lifted a little at the thought of living with Mrs. Brown. He figured that whatever living arrangement she had in mind had to be better than his previous situation. Hell, maybe he could even win her over to where she'd consider adopting him herself, he thought. His hopes, however, were shattered soon after once he found himself in an open dormitory of a group home surrounded by children all with similar backgrounds.

The dorm was set up with bunkbeds standing in straight rows with a day room that held three tables, a ping pong table, and various board games.

Kev estimated that there were close to ten boys present all within five years of his own age. As he sat on his bed contemplating on how abruptly his life had changed, one of the boys approached his bunk and introduced himself as E. "What's up bro? You alright?" the boy asked obviously noticing Kev's bleak look.

Kev looked up at his visitor and gave him a forced smile and a head nod signifying he was okay when he really felt like crying again.

"Alright then. I was just checking up on you 'cause I know how it is your first day in here not knowing anybody and stuff. You're lucky though 'cause we about to have group in about a half hour. You should come."

"Group? What's that?" Kev asked.

"It's a meeting we have with the boys of the dorm where we just talk and go wherever the conversation takes us. It'll be a good place for you to get to know your dorm mates."

Kev wasn't sure if he was ready to fraternize with the others just yet, and E noticed it by the expression he wore on his face.

"It's also a good place to blow off some steam you know, speak what's on your mind. It can be really therapeutic."

Kev heard E's words but didn't really pay much attention to them. His mind had started to wander, and he was thinking about where he was, how long he'd be there, and what exactly it all meant.

"Yo," E said, trying to regain Kev's attention. "You alright? How about I stop by here before it gets started and see if you wanna roll?"

"Yeah, that's cool. Do that."

E departed from Kev's presence, leaving him to brood over the happenings in his life. When he returned, Kev was sitting in the same spot with his eyes held down. He had not moved an inch.

"Damn bro," E said while shaking his head with sympathy. "You got to attend group, it'll make you feel much better, trust me, 'cause I hate to see you like this."

Kev looked up at E then took a deep breath. He needed something, anything. He needed help. He slowly rose to his feet. "Alright man, let's go," he said, effectively bringing a smile to E's face.

Eight boys attended the group session which was held in the activity room. They sat and stood in a semi-circle facing a single chair that was the seat of the moderator whose name was Mr. Griggs.

Mr. Griggs was what everyone called the "Homer Wells" of the group home since he had come there as a baby and had left only once he had turned 18 and was headed off to college. He then returned after earning a doctorate degree in psychology and dedicated his life to helping the youth whose lives were so like his own past. He was black as uncut coffee with snow white teeth and an infectious smile. He was doing what he loved, and it showed by his relations with and responses from his pupils who did their best to emulate him.

As soon as Mr. Griggs saw Kev, he called him by his name, letting him know he already knew who he was, then did his best to make him feel welcomed. At first, Kev only listened to the other boys talk about everything from sports to music to some of the female residents that they had crushes on who stayed in a dorm similar to their own, only downstairs. Their discussion turned more serious once they started talking religion and eventually led to the topic of heaven and hell. When Mr. Griggs asked Kev about his thoughts on the subject, Kev left the gathering speechless after his reply.

"My brother went to hell today," he said, bringing an absolute hush to the room.

Mr. Griggs was visibly taken aback by Kev's answer and was temporarily rendered speechless as he weighed the gravity of it. He finally broke his silence by asking Kev why he thought that was the case.

"Because he did bad things," Kev answered honestly. "I mean, he was a good person and all, but I know that the things he did weren't right."

Mr. Griggs understood Kev's reasoning. Such candid honesty from a boy so young was unnerving and piqued his interest in the wise juvenile. "You know that just because someone has done bad things before, it doesn't necessarily mean that they have to go to hell. Not if they repent for their sins," he said to him.

"What's 'repent'?" Kev asked.

Mr. Griggs took his time and thought before answering. "It's when you genuinely feel sorry for something you've done." His answer depressed Kev even more because now he was certain that his brother was in hell because Craig believed whole heartedly in all of his actions.

Mr. Griggs took notice of Kev's dejection and decided to change the subject before the meeting came to an end so that they could end it on a more positive note. He would sit down and talk to Kev about this more once they were alone.

"That's enough talk about death," he said. "You guys are starting to scare me, besides, y'all too young to be thinking about that stuff anyway. Right now, the only thing y'all need to be concerned with is school and your career choices, so... let me hear them. I don't want to hear what you want to be either, I want to hear what you are going to be, and what you're going to do."

The kids in the group took turns airing their dreams and career aspirations all the way to the conclusion of the meeting without Kev's participation.

Once Kev was back in his bunk, he found himself in the same mood he was in before he went to the session. E must have recognized his emotional state because he didn't come by and bother him for the rest of the night. Kev fell asleep his first night in the group home on top of his covers with his clothes and shoes still on and with troubled thoughts racing through his mind which led to one hellish nightmare.

The next morning, he was awakened by the sound of movement near his bunk. He opened his eyes and saw that most of the boys were up and either walking to or coming from the restroom with toothbrushes in their hands or mouths. He saw E approaching and sat up.

"What up my nigga? You alright?" E asked.

"Yeah, I'm good. What time is it?"

"Around six. They about to run breakfast. You were sleeping good. I was gonna wait 'til the last minute to wake you."

Kev almost laughed at that; his sleep had been restless. He stretched his young muscles with his arms held high over his head.

"Go ahead and get yourself together, then we'll head on down," E said. "Make sure you get all that sleep out your eyes too 'cause the girls will be there."

After washing his face and brushing his teeth and hair, Kev walked down to the cafeteria next to E wearing new clothes which the group home had provided. The cafeteria was a large structure with tables that sat four scattered throughout. Kev and E went through the food line one behind the other and received a breakfast of hotcakes, grits, eggs, orange juice, and milk.

Kev was not used to eating a home cooked breakfast. The only time he got to experience anything close to one would be on the rare occasions his brother got up early to make some money and decided to take him to school. Then they would stop by McDonald's. Other than that, it was almost always cereal.

"They feed us like this every day?" Kev asked.

"Mm-hmm," E answered with a mouthful of pancakes.

Kev was so busy enjoying his meal that he at first failed to take notice of the new guy effect he was having on all the girls who were glancing his way and exchanging whispers. Kev was a handsome young man, brown-skinned with good hair, and dark brown intelligent eyes. One girl specifically caught his eye, and he gave her a head nod and received a slight wave in return. E told him that the girls name was Karma and that she had not been there long and also that all the boys had their eyes on her. He then told Kev the rest of the girls' names and let him know who was dating who.

Kev had temporarily all but forgotten about the drastic events that had transpired the day before as he was getting accustomed to his new life which so far trumped his old one, but once the meal was finished and he was back in his dorm, reality sat in all over again.

E sat next to him on his bunk. "I heard what you said in group yesterday... about your brother. You want to talk about it?"

Kev opened his mouth to reply no, but the word wouldn't come out. He needed to talk about it and decided to. "Man... they just killed him. For no reason at all."

E was about to ask a question but Kev continued. "The police supposed to be on our side, but they shot him." Kev's statement hung in the air.

"You saw it?" E asked in disbelief.

Kev nodded.

"Then you gotta tell somebody what happened. You can't let 'em get away with it."

"Oh yeah, who am I gonna tell, the police?" Kev said sarcastically. E had never thought about it like that, but that's exactly what was going on in the world. The police were investigating themselves for their own crimes. How could one ever expect justice, when that was the process? The police ought to be judged by the people, he thought.

"Then my crackhead mom care more about getting high than she do about her own son. She ain't even come and get me... Its's probably for the best though, 'cause I sure wouldn't have ate a breakfast like that," Kev said, feeling better the more he talked.

"There's nobody else you could go stay with?" E asked.

Kev shook his head no. "What about you?"

"No, I ain't got nobody, never really did," E said, leaving it at that.

The two boys who were the same age and in the same predicament sat silent on the bunk for a few minutes.

"It's not that bad here. You'll see, it's actually better off than a lot of us was living before. They feed us good, as you already saw. We go on field trips, got good teachers and they give us new clothes."

The mention of clothes made Kev remember the ones he had changed out of which his brother had bought for him. He made a mental note to keep them forever in remembrance of Craig. As he thought about the old clothes, he remembered the sack of rocks that he still had stashed in his briefs. He briefly entertained the idea of throwing them away since he knew he'd be in big trouble if he got caught with them, but then he remembered Craig telling him that the rocks were money and that money could get him anything, so he decided to keep them. He wasn't sure exactly how he would turn them into cash, but he knew that eventually, he would.

CHAPTER 3

As weeks went by, Kev saw that E was right and that the program wasn't that bad. He missed his brother Craig more than ever, and he even missed his mom a little too, but all in all he was as happy as he could ever remember. His friendship with E had strengthened tremendously over time and provided them both comfort whenever they started feeling down. Karma was proving to be a godsend. She and Kev just seemed to get along effortlessly. They started off just conversing with each other whenever an opportunity presented itself, to eventually pairing up for every activity or field trip. E was still his boy and best friend, but Karma was now his girlfriend. They shared their first kiss on the day that she was leaving the group home to stay with a relative who had gained legal custody, and it was tough for the both of them.

"Will you write me?" Kev had asked once their lips separated

"Of course I'll write you silly. I'll visit too. That wasn't a goodbye kiss Kev, that was an 'I love you' kiss."

That was the first time she had told him that, and as he thought about it, it was the first time anyone had told him those three words as far as he could remember. Hearing them made his heart swell up in his chest.

"I love you too," he said in return.

"Don't say it just because I said it," Karma said. "Say it only if you mean it."

"I do mean it."

She kissed him again and pressed her body against his this time. Kev felt her small breasts press against him, along with her pelvis as she grinded her body against his. When his manhood grew hard, he stopped kissing her and pulled away. Karma smiled a tender knowing smile. She knew he was scared to go all the way with it because she was too. They were both still virgins, but the difference was she was ready and willing.

"Don't worry," she said noticing the fear of disappointment in his eyes. "I'll wait for you."

Kev exhaled a sigh of relief. As always, she said exactly what he needed to hear. When she left later that day, Kev was understandably battling mixed emotions. As much as it hurt him that she was leaving, he was just as happy to see her go. After Karma's departure, Kev's relationship with Mr. Griggs also blossomed into something substantial. The charismatic counselor seemed to take special interest in Kev, and the two of them frequently carried on their group conversations well after the others had left. Kev's direct simplistic approach to even the most sophisticated of problems gave Mr. Griggs a clarity that even world-renowned philosophers failed to achieve. When Mr. Griggs asked him about his future plans, like he always did, he was shocked when Kev told him that everyone's future wasn't going to be bright.

"Why do you say that?" Mr. Griggs asked.

Kev shrugged his shoulders. "I just don't think everyone wants to grow old."

"What about you Kevin, don't you want to grow old and have children and grandchildren?"

Kev scratched his head as he thought about an answer. "No... Not really."

After hearing that answer, Mr. Griggs made a vow to himself to do his absolute best and to go the extra mile to improve this young man's life and to get him on the path to success. He told him that he'd always be there for him and he meant it.

Kev was doing good in the program. He was participating in all the activities and had moved into a leadership role helping mentor and tutor some of the other kids.

His demeanor grew jovial, and his level of maturity seemed to soar above the rest along with his grades. When Mr. Griggs came to him six months later and told him that he had found him a home, Kev didn't know whether to be happy or sad. He had grown so accustomed to his surroundings that he didn't want to leave. "Do I gotta go?" He asked Mr. Griggs as the two of them sat in his office.

"You should want to go. I know you've settled in here, but trust me, this isn't what's up. You need a real family environment." Kev still looked disappointed.

"Don't you trust me, Kev?"

Kev nodded his head.

"Then you know that I'd never steer you wrong. The Johnsons are a good middle-class family that'll bless you with opportunities that most Black kids don't have."

Kev knew that Mr. Griggs was telling the truth, and that this was indeed a blessing. He was just feeling guilty about leaving all his friends behind, E most of all. E, however, seemed fine with the news, even happy for Kev.

"Man, you'll probably get to go to college and everything now," E said as he helped Kev pack his belongings.

"I ain't going to no college E."

"What? You tripping Kev. Why you acting all sad? You should be happy."

"Oh yeah, and why is that?"

"Cause you getting up out of here," E said as if it should have been obvious.

"Just swapping out one set of rules for another… and probably stricter too. I'm telling you now, if it ain't right, I'm skippin'."

E stopped what he was doing and looked Kev in the eyes. He was thinking how Kev was not appreciating the situation. "Well if you do decide to skip, put in a good word for me, I wouldn't care if they were the Parkers."

"Who is the Parkers?" Kev asked.

"You know, Family Guy."

Kev smiled and shook his head. "Now that's a messed up family."

The Johnsons turned out to be more like the Huxtables rather than the Parkers though. They seemed like a family straight off the cover of Ebony magazine. Mr. Johnson was a small light-skinned middle-aged Black man with pork chop sideburns, and round wire-rimmed glasses. He worked as an editor for the local newspaper and looked every bit the part. Mrs. Johnson was the same size and complexion as her husband and could have easily passed for his sister. If it wasn't for her well-developed protruding breasts, she just as well may have passed for his brother instead. She was a dental hygienist and was obviously the one who set the rules for the household. Their son's name was Martin and although he was Kev's age, he either didn't like to talk much or just didn't like Kev, because after their initial introduction, he said nothing.

The Johnsons lived in a nice three-bedroom home in the Firestone area and had two cars parked in their garage, Mr. Johnson's Ford Explorer and Mrs. Johnson's Volvo. Kev immediately felt uncomfortable. Every time they spoke, and every action they took seemed foreign and weird to him. He couldn't believe that they only had one TV in the house, but he was even more amazed to find out that it didn't have cable and was only used to watch movies together as a family on the weekends. Kev felt that was a little extreme, but he understood what they were trying to do, so he figured he could manage. It wasn't until later that evening when dinner was served that Kev knew that this setup wasn't going to work. The dinner itself was fabulous. They had spaghetti and meatballs paired with salad and garlic bread. After Mr. Johnson said the grace, blessing the food, Kev picked up a fork and started digging into the spaghetti.

When Martin started chuckling, Kev had no idea that it was directed towards him; but when he looked up at the boy and Martin rolled his eyes, smirked, and shook his head. There was no doubt about who he was laughing at.

Kev put his fork back down on the table. "What's so funny?" he asked the boy only to have Mrs. Johnson cut in. "You'll have to excuse Martin's poor manners Kevin, but the reason he's acting like that is because that's your salad fork, you're eating with."

At first Kev felt relieved because he had thought Martin was laughing at his appetite. That feeling of relief however quickly turned into first embarrassment and then anger once Kev thought over the situation. Just like that he knew that he did not belong in this house, and also that he wouldn't stay there. People like the Johnsons were good people with genuine good intentions, Kev thought, but they were the family his brother would have referred to as growing up on the other side of the tracks. They were perfect in his eyes. Kev wasn't and didn't believe he ever would be.

* * *

Later that night, while everyone was sleeping, Kev packed his backpack with his personal belongings and then snuck out of the house. As he walked the city streets alone at two in the morning, he felt no fear. Instead what he felt was a mixture of anxiety and euphoria because he knew where he was headed—he was going home. The trek from the Johnsons' house to his home on Greenwood took Kev a little over an hour. When his house came into view, he was amazed to see it buzzing with activity. There were people milling around the lawn and front porch, and when Kev approached, one of the strangers extended a twenty-dollar bill towards him. "You on?" The crackhead asked.

Kev was taken by surprise, but he remained calm and nodded his head, acting like it was the norm. He took the twenty then took off his backpack and rummaged through it. When he found what he was looking for, which was his brother's sack of rocks, he kept them out of view of the man then removed one from the bag and placed it in the customer's hand. All the time he had spent in silence watching his brother work had taught him the game. He knew it better than any test he'd ever take in school.

When some of the other smokers who were either standing around or sitting on the porch saw that Kev had served the man right, they started approaching him with whatever money they had. Some had tens, some had twenties, one had a one-hundred-dollar bill, and more than a few had change. Kev served them all. He remembered his brother had told him that "he never let no money walk away because it all added up." A few of the customers complained about the size of their purchase, but Kev knew what he was doing, and everyone got exactly what they had paid for. There was no overs and no love. Craig didn't give the game a black eye and neither would he.

After he had finished serving everybody, he noticed that the entire crowd had dispersed and that he was now standing outside alone. Even though it was dark out, Kev could still notice all the changes his home had gone through in the time he was gone. The front lawn was no longer green grass but instead just hardened dusty brown dirt. The steps to the front porch looked to be coming detached from the house and the banister leaned dangerously outward. When he entered the house, it was pitch black inside with the only illumination coming from the rose of fire coming from the stems of crack pipes. Kev could discern the silhouettes of people sitting on couches, chairs, and crates, also the ones lying on the floor and against the wall.

Not thinking he made his way to the light switch and tried to flick it up, but discovered it was already in the upward position.

"Kevin?" a voice called out from the darkness.

Kev recognized it as his mother's voice at once and whirled around to locate her. Even after all the pain she had caused him, she was still his mother and the sound of her voice alone brought him joy.

"Mom?"

A disheveled apparition of a person appeared at his side making him take a step back.

"Mom, I've been—"

"Is you the one they said was on?" Brenda asked.

Kev stood astonished with his head slightly tilted to the side. He slowly started shaking his head in disbelief at how unconcerned she was about his welfare. He realized though that he should not be surprised. Craig had told him that she didn't care about anything other than getting high and like everything else Craig had told him, this seemed true also. Kev's joy dissipated like fog being entered and he answered flatly.

"Yeah, I'm straight, you got some money?"

"No, but I'm your mom," Brenda said, as if that were enough then added. "And this is my house and..."

Before she could finish her sentence, Kev had extracted a rock and placed it in her hand then turned and started feeling his way upstairs feeling disgusted. When he entered his old room, he saw there were people laying on the floor and in his bed.

"Y'all got to get out of here, this is my room," Kev said with as much authority in his voice his small frame could muster.

The occupants stirred then started getting up and leaving with no protest. After waking and delivering his message to a few others, he once again had his room to himself.

Now that he had accomplished everything, he had set out to do this night he didn't know what to do next. As reality set in about his life's circumstances, he felt a rush of emotion and started crying a silent cry with a steady flow of tears. A thought of his brother Craig made his tears stop flowing. He had never seen Craig cry, and although Craig had been older than himself, he had never not once cried about their situation. In fact, Craig did whatever was necessary to make the best of his situation, and he knew that meant getting money and making sure he had everything he needed from here on out. As he thought about it, a smile spread across his face, he knew he could do it, and also that he might even have some fun while he was at it. He found a corner and hunched down in it just as a light rapping came from the door.

"Come in," he said in his new voice of authority.

As Kev watched the stranger enter his room with a crumpled-up fist full of dollars, he knew it would be a long sleepless night, but also a profitable one.

CHAPTER 4

At daybreak, Kev was sitting in his room alone counting his money.

"Eight-hundred forty-seven dollars and seventy-five cents," he said to himself.

He could not believe it. He had started last night off with five dollars to his name and now what he was looking at was a small fortune to him. He stacked the money up neatly with all the bills facing the same way and in order of their denominations with the ones on top all the way to the hundreds which were on the bottom.

After folding the money up, he placed a rubber band on the knot then hid it in the pocket of his briefs. After putting all the change he had accumulated in a sandwich bag and placing it in his backpack, he took out his sack of rocks. The baggie that had held over fifty rocks in it, now held only twelve. It had indeed been a busy night. When Kev heard a knock at the door, he put a quick knot in the bag then put it in his pocket before telling his visitor to come in. He knew that the person knocking was Reka because they had established a system the night before where she would be the only one he served so he would not have to deal with all the riff raff and haggling. Nobody else, not even his mother was to do business with him. Reka had explained to him that it would not be busy like that every night; that it was only because it was the first of the month and people had gotten their welfare checks, and the usual pusher had garbage product at the moment.

"Good morning, Kevin," she said, a little too chipper as she entered the room.

"Kev, Reka. Call me Kev... and good morning to you, too."

"Don't be a grouch, baby... and besides, I come with good news."

"Oh yeah? What's up?"

"Well, first I need you to put something together for this fifty..." she said then handed Kev a fifty-dollar bill. "And then the man who this belongs to is willing to let us use his car half the day for another fifty."

This was good news to Kev. He already had a lot planned on what all he wanted to do today.

"Okay, that's what's up," he said, then gave Reka the drugs and watched as she broke a small piece off and put it in her own bag. "I got to get washed up first then I'll be ready," he finished.

"You gon' have to do that on the road baby 'cause ain't no hot water here. Don't worry about it though, we'll stop over a friend of mine's. Let me go handle this, then I'll be ready.

Kev stood up and stretched then walked to the bathroom and pissed in a toilet that was in worse shape than any port-o-potty he had ever seen. After handling his business, he walked downstairs to join Reka, leaving his backpack in his room. Reka held up the car keys when she saw him, then the two of them left.

The man's car was an old 1996 Chevy Lumina with tinted windows and two missing hubcaps. The inside of the car smelled like old tennis shoes and cigarettes, and the backseat was strewn with trash, but the engine was strong, and it would suffice in getting them where they needed to go. Reka took him to some fat man's house so he could take a shower while she and the fat man went and "talked" in the guy's bedroom. Once Kev was all cleaned up and they were back in the car, he turned to Reka.

"Who was that fat dude?"

"Who? Earl? Earl ain't nobody but a trick. Just a big, fat, greasy trick; but his money is green, and he don't mind parting with it for your auntie."

For some unknown reason this made Kev upset. He did not know why but he was feeling possessive over Reka.

"You ain't gotta do that no more," he said.

"Do what?"

Kev hesitated before answering. "You ain't gotta mess wit nobody for no money no more. You wit me now and I'mma keep you straight."

His statement hit Reka hard and she had to turn her face away so he wouldn't see her tear up. She had been doing favors for men in exchange for money since she was fourteen and never once had one told her to stop. Now, here was a thirteen-year-old kid telling her she didn't have to do it anymore, and what was even stranger, was that she believed him. He had no way of knowing it, but Reka secretly pledged her allegiance and loyalty to him for life, right there in that moment.

"Okay, where we headed?" she asked, breaking the silence that hung in the air as she turned the car on Main Street.

"First, Home Depot, then the mall and grocery store. I need you to get the utilities cut on in the house, too. I got the money, just tell me how much we need 'cause we can't keep living like that."

Reka was blown away but did not let it show. It was like she was watching Kev become a man right before her eyes, he reminded her of Craig. "I can handle that. We'll just put them in somebody else's name," she answered. "Anything else you need me to do?"

"Yeah, get somebody to clean and fix the house up. Make it look presentable."

"You just buy some cleaning supplies and I'll do all the cleaning. Plenty of your customers are handymen who'll practically build you a new house for some crumbs, so that won't be a problem either."

At the Home Depot, Kev bought the necessary cleaning supplies along with candles, grass seed, hay, portable refrigerator, an air mattress, and a dead bolt lock for his bedroom door. When they went to the mall, he purchased both him and Karma a pair of matching tennis shoes along with outfits, then they went to the grocery store and bought all his favorite foods. The rest of the day went by in a blur to Kev. Reka indeed managed to get the utilities cut on and clean the place up too. The house was already starting to look better in just a day's work. After Kev had the lock installed on his bedroom door, he locked it then walked over to the baseboard where he knew Craig kept his stash. Kev had left his backpack in the room when they left on purpose just to test his mother's will. He had left her instructions not to let anyone in his room, but of course, when he had returned, his backpack had been emptied and his change was gone.

Anyone could have stolen it, but he knew it was his mother. He laughed at it though, now it was official that she was dead to him, and besides, this new lock and Craig's stash spot would be enough to keep him from getting ripped off again.

He removed the baseboard from the wall exposing the hole, then stuck his hand in and felt around the floor until he felt cold steel. He pulled the object out of the wall and saw that he was holding a 380-Caliber Berretta handgun. Kev had never used a gun before, but between video games and watching Craig, he had a fairly good idea how it worked. He slid the clip out discovering that the firearm was fully loaded, then slid it back in. After placing the gun on the floor next to him, he stuck his arm back in the hole and this time, retrieved a large zip-lock bag containing money and a white powdery substance. He took the money out first which was all hundred-dollar bills bundled in one rubber band, sixty-five in total.

"Cha-ching," he said aloud to himself then proceeded to counting the money before placing it back in the bag and removing the bag of powder which was three separate bags inside of one.

Kev already knew that the white powder was cocaine, and also that it was the stuff that made crack. This time when he stuck his hand back in the hole, it did not take long for him to locate the digital scale he was seeking. He turned the scale on and weighed each of the three bags of cocaine and saw that each one weighed 29.1 grams. Now he figured all he had to do was get Reka to show him how to turn it into crack and his diminished cache of rocks problem would be solved.

Later that night when he showed her two of the ounces of powder, her eyes got buggy and she licked her lips.

"Where in the world did you get all this work you been having?" she asked.

Kev just smirked.

"You know what, I don't even wanna know, and I just hope you didn't rob nobody or nothing like that."

Now Kev shook his head. "Na don't worry. I ain't did nothing. Craig left it to me."

Craig's name brought back memories to the both of them.

"What?" Kev asked after noticing Reka shaking her head.

"Nothing. It's just amazing that your big bro is still managing to look after you even after he's gone. That's alright... what you want me to do with that though? I could try to sell it, but there ain't no powder customers coming through here."

"No, I want you to make it turn into crack."

"Who me? I don't know how to cook, Kev, but I do know somebody who does. He gon' charge you though."

She took him to some light-skinned guy named Fred's house. Fred had a mouth full of gold teeth, a white Cadillac Escalade, a DTS, and he wore two gold chains around his neck which both held diamond encrusted medallions. His girl Mel cooked the dope while Kev and Reka waited and chatted with Fred.

"So, you Craig's lil brother," Fred said after blowing out a huge cloud of marijuana smoke.

Kev only nodded in response.

"That's what's up. It's fucked up what those pussy ass crooked cops did to my boy. We should've burned this bitch down like they did in Ferguson."

"You knew my brother?"

"Hell yeah, we was tight. We went to school together and everything. I used to sell him all his work."

Another problem solved Kev thought. Now he knew where to come when he ran out of product.

Just then, Fred's girlfriend Mel came in the room carrying two sandwich baggies with a rock hard perfectly round white cookie in each one and handed them both to Kev. She then walked seductively over to Fred and kissed him on the cheek before sitting on his lap. The spandex pants, she wore left little to the imagination and had Kev wishing it was his lap she was sitting on.

"Now, when I tell you my baby the truth, I mean that shit," Fred said, then hit the blunt twice more before passing it to Mel.

"Put that shit on the scale and see what it's weighing up at."

There was a digital scale sitting on the coffee table in front of Kev, who did as he was told and placed one of the cookies on top of it. It weighed 37.5 grams without the bag, and the other one weighed an even 38.

"Proper, ain't it?" Fred said with a smile flashing his eight open-faced gold permanents.

"Yeah, it's A1," Kev answered. "What I owe you?"

"That's on the house since you Craig lil bro, just make sure you come see me when you tryna cop some more."

"Alright, bet," Kev said, preparing to leave but stopping as he remembered what his brother used to tell him about despising a free meal, and never taking handouts. Not wanting to offend, he thought of a way to get around it.

"You mind if I tip the cook?" he asked.

Fred nodded his head giving him permission.

Kev handed Mel a one-hundred-dollar bill with a smile. "Thank you," he said bashfully.

Mel took the bill and put it in her bra. "Aww no problem, sweetie," she said then leaned forward and placed a kiss on his cheek making him blush.

Kev and Reka said their goodbyes then walked out of Fred's house and got in the car to head home. Kev sat in quiet contemplation on the ride back. Mel's kiss had made him think of Karma and their first kiss.

It bothered him that he did not know how to be with a girl without feeling all funny inside. Later that night when the traffic had slowed down, he called Reka up to his room. "I need your help with something," he said once she had sat down.

"What's up?"

Kev stared at a spot on the floor instead of continuing.

"What's on your mind, Kev?" He started to change his mind and just say forget it, but something told him that this was the right course of action, so he went through with it. "I... I need you to tell me how to be with a girl."

Reka smiled, he had surprised her. "I'll do even better. I'll show you how to be with a woman," she said, then stood up and sat next to him on the bed.

She freed one of her large breasts from her shirt to Kev's dismay. "What you doin'?" he asked, trying to retreat, but never taking his eyes off her brown nipple.

"Listen, Kev. I could tell you how to make me feel good, but it would only go in one ear and out the other. The only way to learn how to please a woman is to please one, now suck on this," she raised her breast up as if offering.

Kev hesitated at first, then leaned in and latched on.

"No, no, no," Reka said, pulling her nipple free from his mouth.

"Start slowly, first start kissing my neck and work your way down and hold it with your hand and caress it."

Kev did as he was told and started kissing her neck while gently squeezing her tit and nipple. His dick instantly got rock hard.

"Good, good... yeah, that feels good. Now suck on it and remember no teeth."

Kev started sucking on her nipple again, this time going slowly, using only his lips and tongue.

Reka knew that what she was doing was wrong, but the thought that he'd always have drugs for her was enough to make this seem like an opportune chance. She knew that once she put it on him, he'd come back again and again, just like everyone else. Besides, it wasn't like she was hurting him.

She took his hand and placed it on her other breast.

"Rub on it, Kev. Squeeze it... pull it. You see how the nipple gets hard. Now suck on that one... that's right, you making my pussy wet now." She took his hand and slid it inside her pants so he could feel her slick pussy. "You ready for some pussy, Kev?"

Kev couldn't talk with her titty in his mouth, so he just mumbled his response. "Mmmhmm." He liked it.

Reka pulled his head off her chest, then slid her pants and panties off and laid back on the bed.

"Take your clothes off," she instructed.

He followed her instructions even though he was embarrassed by his nakedness.

"Now come here," she beckoned as she spread her legs open like the wings of a butterfly.

When Kev got close enough, she reached out and grabbed ahold of his swollen penis and pulled him closer. She then guided him inside of her. He instinctively thrust his hips forward, diving deeper into her core while gripping on her ass cheeks. "That's it... that's it, Kev, you make me feel good. Grind on my pussy, baby."

The warmth of being inside Reka made Kev want to burrow deeper. In just a few minutes, he felt his body shudder, then an energy start to flow through him and out of his manhood he'd never felt before, but already wanted to feel again, and as much as possible.

"Okay, now beat it up. Beat the pussy like you tryna hurt it, until it all comes out," she said, then used her hands to guide his hips showing him the motion and pace she desired.

Kev bucked repeatedly and watched as her titties bounced to the rhythm. His load flowed out of him and into her like a current. Once it was over, he collapsed on top of her while still inside. She rubbed the back of his head lovingly then lifted her breast to his mouth once more. "Here baby, take this," she said, pressing her nipple to his lips. "Tomorrow, I'm going to suck on you," she promised, knowing that he would melt in her mouth and be her puppet after that.

CHAPTER 5

Kev could not believe his eyes. Although he was sitting on the steps waiting for his boy to come over, seeing him walking up the street made it a reality.

"E! What up my nigga?" he said, as soon as E was within twenty feet.

E smiled as he closed the distance between the two of them. When he reached the porch, he and Kev shared a brotherly hug. "You called, I came," he said of Kev's invitation.

"Yeah man, ain't no reason for you to be staying in no group home when yo boy got his own crib."

"Nigga this ain't yours."

"Might as well be, I pay the bills and got it fixed up. You should have saw it the first night I came back, it looked like Michael Myers' crib or something. I was almost scared to go in."

In the six months that Kev had been back home, the house had made a complete transformation. The porch was fixed, it now had green grass growing. It was painted, had a new front door, and was in the process of getting a roof put on as they spoke.

"So, you hustling that good, huh?"

Before Kev could answer, Reka came out of the house and onto the front porch looking as if she had made a complete transformation, also. Her hair and nails were done and she wore new clothes and tennis shoes. She was still getting high, but with all her thickness and curves returning one would have never guessed it. "I need to holler at you for a second."

"Alright, this my friend E I was telling you about," Kev said.

Reka smiled and spoke to E, then Kev got up to follow her into the house and told E he'd be right back. Kev and Reka's relationship was complex. It was business, sexual, personal, and strangely maternal, but somehow managed to work; they both were happy. He returned to the porch after a few minutes and sat back down next to E on the steps.

"So, who is she?" E asked, talking about Reka.

"That's my home girl. She be helping me get this money."

"Damn, she's fine as hell. She live here too?"

"Yep."

"Oh yeah? How Karma feel about that?"

Kev just looked at him and shook his head. Karma hated Reka and didn't hide it.

"That bad, huh? Where Karma at anyway? I thought she'd be here."

"She's at school. She'll be over later. We got some business to handle before she get out though."

"What you got in mind, bro?"

Kev started to answer but changed his mind. "It's a surprise. Its gon' blow your mind though. Come on, let's go."

Kev got up and went in the house to get Reka. When they came back outside, the three of them got in a Dodge Charger rental car and left. Kev drove them to the Eastside of Akron, to a housing project off of Wilbeth Road. E laughed at him the whole ride over because Kev was so small sitting behind the wheel that he had to sit on pillows in order not to stand out. Once they arrived at their destination however, E stopped laughing.

"What business you got over here?" E asked as he surveyed the housing project.

Kev knew what was bothering him. It was simple, E was a Crip, and this was a Blood neighborhood. Kev reached over across Reka's lap and opened the glove box and took out his pistol. "Be careful with that thing," Reka said. "I don't know why you brought it anyway."

"Because it's better to have it and not need it than need it and not have it," Kev answered the same as he'd always heard Craig respond.

"What business you got over here?" E repeated.

Kev almost laughed and called him scary. "I'm 'bout to buy a car from one of these niggas," Kev finally answered, as he tucked his pistol in his waistband then got out of the car.

E and Reka got out after Kev and followed him to one of the apartments. As they were walking, E noticed an all black 1985 Buick Regal with tinted windows and 24-inch chrome rims in the parking lot with for sale signs in the front and back windows.

"Nigga, tell me you about to buy that Regal?" E said with excitement as they approached the door.

Kev smiled then knocked on the door. As soon as the door was opened, a wave of rap music and weed smoke flooded across the threshold. A heavyset Black man stood in the doorway wearing a white wifebeater and black jeans with a designer red belt and an all red Cleveland Indians hat.

"What's good?" the man said while staring at Reka.

"What's up bro, I came to see about that Regal for sale. I called earlier. Is it yours?"

The man's name was Rodney and he remembered talking to Kev about the car. "You really wanna buy it?" Rodney said in disbelief, stressing the word, you.

"I'm thinking about it, you mind showing it to me?"

Rodney gave Kev a look like he was impressed and nodded his head in approval. He excused himself and went back inside to retrieve the cars keys. When he came back out, the quartet walked to the car together.

"How old is you, Kev?"

"Fourteen."

"... and you got five racks to spend on a car?"

"I licked the dice game," Kev lied.

"Damn, you's a lucky muthafucka... and you gon' spend it all on a whip?"

"You only live once," Kev answered properly.

They reached the car and Rodney pressed a button on the remote that unlocked the doors and made the alarm chirp twice, disarming itself.

"This was my baby, here," Rodney said, opening the door so his guest could look inside.

The inside of the car was just as clean as the outside. It had gray leather seats, a wood-grain steering wheel, the shifter was in the floor and there was even an infotainment monitor.

"This is dope," Reka said, unable to contain her excitement.

"Start it up," Rodney said.

Kev took the keys and cranked the engine up, which turned over easily on the first try and gave off a deep rumbling sound.

"It's got a 350 rocket with low miles, dual exhaust, and a posi rear end which means both tires gon' spin when you burn out. Plus, a proper sound system," Rodney said, and patted the car like a proud father. "You get everything in the package."

Kev had initially planned to try to negotiate Rodney down to $4500 at most, but after Rodney's display, he decided to give the man what he was asking.

"I'm sold, man. You got yourself a deal," Kev said, then pulled out a big bankroll.

They went to the DMV on Tallmadge Road where Rodney put the title of the car in Reka's name. Kev had Reka drive the rental home while him and E rolled down Interstate 76 back to the West side in the new whip.

"Where we headed now?" E asked.

Kev looked at his watch. "We still got a few hours before Karma gets out of school. We might as well just ride 'til then."

They got off the interstate by Hawkins Plaza and rode along listening to music. After a couple of songs played, Kev picked up the remote and turned the music down. "So, what you wanna do, E? You wanna stay at the house with me and get this money, or we going back?"

E looked at Kev like he had two heads. "Nigga what type of question is that! You know I ain't going back."

"Cool, that's what's up. That means we brothers now."

"Fo' life," E added, liking the sound of it. He had never had a brother, and when Kev said it, he eagerly welcomed it.

Kev turned the car on Frederick Street and they both spotted some young ladies standing outside a house, milling around. "Pull over there, Kev. Pull up to the curb," E urged.

Kev pulled the car up to the curb in front of the house and all the girls turned their attention to them to see who their visitors were. They seemed to be a little older than both Kev and E, but Kev and E weren't intimidated, because the car gave them confidence.

E pressed a button, making his window slide down, then beckoned for one of the girls to come here. Three of the young ladies approached the car.

"What's up?" E said, then told the girls his name and introduced Kev who just sat there watching.

The three girls introduced themselves in return as Erica, Tiffany, and Jasmine and then looked the car over. "Whose car is this?" the girl named Erica asked

"This is my car," Kev spoke up.

Erica walked around the car to Kev's window which he let down.

"How old are you?" she asked, leaning on the windowsill.

"I'm fourteen," Kev answered, then asked how old she was. She said she was sixteen.

"You didn't steal this car, did you?" she asked, taking a step back as the other girls and E just watched and listened.

"Nope, I just bought it today," Kev said proudly.

Erica returned to her position on the windowsill. "Is that why you ain't in school?" she asked.

Kev chuckled. "Na, I already graduated," he said, then laughed out loud.

Erica didn't laugh. "You ain't graduated, you too young. You probably dropped out like everybody else."

"I'm for real, I just graduated from a different type of school," Kev said seriously.

"... and what type is that?"

"The School of Hard Knocks."

Erica actually liked that answer. She knew it meant he was a hustler and street nigga.

"Why ain't y'all in school?" Kev asked.

"We havin' a party here tonight and we had to get ready. You and yo' boy should come."

Kev turned to E who was engaged in a conversation with the girl named Tiffany. "How 'bout it E, you wanna slide to their party tonight?"

E looked at Kev sideways yet again. "Now that's the second crazy question you've asked."

Kev started laughing then turned back to Erica. "We'll be there."

They conversed a little more then got the girls phone numbers then pulled off. E was giddy.

"Man, Tiffany said she was seventeen. She's a senior, man. This car a hoe magnet... Man bro, this might be the best day of my life," E said.

Kev smiled. That's exactly why he had invited E to stay with him. He wanted to change his life for the better and replace some of that pain with joy.

When they left from talking to the girls, it was just about time for Karma to get out of school. She didn't know about him purchasing the car, and he was planning on surprising her by picking her up in it. He was purposely late getting there and caught up with her and her girls walking down Winton Street. He turned the music up as his car approached.

"Womp! womp! womp!" The bass blasted loud enough from his subwoofers to make all the girls turn around and see where it was coming from. All of them but Karma—she never looked back. Kev coasted the car up next to them and slowed down to the pace they were walking. He cut the music down first then rolled down the passenger window. Now, the whole group of girls had stopped walking to see who it was, Karma included.

"Which one of y'all is named Karma?" Kev asked trying to disguise his voice, but laughing.

As soon as she heard his voice, she recognized E in the passenger seat grinning from ear to ear

"Kevin," she said then walked up to the car.

E opened the door and got out and spoke, then climbed in the back seat so Karma could sit up front.

"Ask yo girl if she wanna ride," E said before she closed the door.

Karma's girl friend didn't hesitate or wait to be asked. She quickly slid in the backseat next to E, smiling the whole time. Karma gave Kev a kiss on the cheek after closing the door. "Whose car is this?" She asked him.

"It's ours."

Karma got quiet as if thinking and her face grew serious. "I don't like it."

Kev was shocked. "You don't?"

"It's nice looking and all, but it's just a little too much... I thought with what you do, you wouldn't want people to see you."

Karma was thinking of the police, jack boys, and most of all other girls, who would all now have him on their radars. What was so crazy was that her views just showed the difference in the way a man and woman think, because that's exactly why Kev had bought it—to be seen.

"Well, it's all good," Kev said, not knowing what else to say, then decided to change the subject. "Y'all hungry?" he asked everyone in the car and received enthusiastic yesses from all.

They went to his favorite spot to eat, which was a drive-in restaurant that served you by running your food out to your car and was famous for their shakes and burgers.

"Now, I ain't even got to say that if anybody drop a crumb in my car, all y'all walking," Kev said, then started laughing, even though he was serious.

"You'd make me walk, too?" Karma said, then made a sad puppy dog face.

Kev didn't hesitate. "All the way from the moon."

Karma acted shocked, then playfully pushed the side of his head.

After eating their food, Kev dropped Karma's friend off at her house first then took Karma home. Karma made him stop at the corner of the street she lived on. "Un-un. My aunt would kill me if she seen me get out of this car," she said when Kev tried to insist on pulling up to the house. "I especially don't want her to know you bought it, she'd have a thousand questions and I'd have to think of a thousand lies. I'll call you in a couple of hours and you can come pick me up from Ebony's, okay?" she said then gave him a kiss before getting out of the car and scampering up the street.

Kev spent the next few hours, before Karma's call would come, teaching E the dope game.

"Look, it's easy..." Kev said. "These are dimes, and these are twenties." Kev showed him two different sized rocks. He showed him how to make and cut deals and how to move. Everything else added up. "If you run across somebody asking you for a double up or an 8-ball or better, just call me. It's really easy because the dope sells itself, all you got to do is have it, and I stay wit it. So you gon' be straight." E looked and listened as if he understood.

"You got it?" Kev asked looking for a little reassurance before he parted with his product.

"Yea, I should be good," E said, lacking the confidence Kev was looking for.

Kev's cell phone rang, he saw that it was Karma, and answered. "Okay, you ready?" he said, then listened to her reply. "Alright, I'll be there in a minute."

After ending the call, he turned his attention back to E. "Take this," he handed E a sandwich bag full of rocks of various sizes. "That's half an ounce right there. Just bring me back $700. I don't care how you sell it, just make sure the money straight and we good. But remember, you wanna make your profit too, so be smart and get yo money."

E pocketed the drugs. "I appreciate it Kev. You a real one," he said, then dapped Kev up.

"It ain't nothing, just doing what I'm supposed to do." Kev said.

"Look, I gotta go pick up Karma. I want you to hold the spot down until I get back. When I do, I'mma have Reka take you to this house down in the valley where you can stay. It's a duplex and I rented you a room. It's a whole lotta money in that hood to be made but it's hot, and the niggas is deadly." Kev was speaking of a rough neighborhood on the Westside they called the valley, or "the V" for short. E nodded his head showing that he understood, and Kev left, but returned shortly with Karma in tow.

E noticed that Karma and Reka didn't speak to each other and the look they exchanged was anything but friendly.

"Say Reka, you can take E to the spot on Haynes now and stay with him and get him a few customers coming through, okay?"

Reka watched as Kev led Karma upstairs not waiting on her reply. She knew they had been fucking like rabbits and she had told Kev not to get her pregnant and to wear protection, but she seriously doubted he was listening. It was her own secret satisfaction though, that she knew that whatever Kev was doing to Karma, he had done to her already and was still doing it.

So, as she watched Karma switch her hips up the stairs she felt a small bit of jealousy but also a huge sense of satisfaction.

Once Kev and Karma were inside Kev's room, he locked the door then went and joined Karma on the bed and laid back as she used the remote to flip through channels on the TV. Reka had taught him to be patient with women. She had explained to him that Karma's hormones were going just as crazy as his, and all that he had to do was look good and wait and that Karma would eventually, let it be known what she wanted to do. He sat back and stared at her delicate profile as she watched TV. Karma was a mulatto girl with long brown hair. She looked up from the TV and caught Kev staring. "What?" she asked, then flashed a smile showing off a set of perfect white teeth.

"Just looking at how beautiful you are, and thinking about how lucky I am."

"Aww, that's so sweet." She kissed him on the lips and snuggled closer to his body.

Kev wrapped his arm around her waist and lay there waiting. Karma kissed his cheek then his lips. When he reached his hand down between her legs and lightly rubbed her vagina, she let out a small gasp then started kissing him hard with her tongue leading the way. He could feel her nipples pushing into his chest, making him rock hard. When she felt his erection pressing through his pants, she grinded against it, and her love started getting wet, and he could feel its wetness on his fingers through her shorts. They kissed and made love with passion because it was in their hearts. They had been doing this same routine every day since Reka had schooled Kev, and Karma was already six weeks pregnant but hadn't told anyone yet.

Just as Kev started coming inside of her he heard a light rapping on his bedroom door.

"Kevin! Kevin open the door. Open the goddamn door."

He got up, put on some jeans and went and opened the door. His mother stood in front of him. She looked over his shoulder and saw Karma curled up under the bedsheet looking right back at her.

"You think you gon' lay up in my house all day making money and fucking that lil hoe, you got another thing com—" She stopped short when she saw the rock in Kev's hand.

"You ain't got to scheme every time Karma comes over, Brenda, you know I be looking out for you," he said then dropped the rock in her hand.

She ignored his statement and placed the rock in her mouth. "You gon' get that girl pregnant... watch and see, then yo ass gon' be in trouble. She gon' leave yo ass one day, watch and—"

"I'll be alright," he said, then closed and locked the door.

He walked back to the bed and watched as Karma removed the sheet exposing her naked body. Kev stared at her admirably then climbed up on the bed and placed his face between her legs, doing exactly as he was taught.

CHAPTER 6

After Kev and Karma were through expressing their teenage passions, Kev took her home, then went to the spot on Haynes to check on E.

"How you like your spot?" he asked as he entered the house.

"Man, Kev, I can't thank you enough bro, got a room a kitchen and a bathroom. I'm good," E responded. Him and Reka were sitting in the living room watching a hood movie on YouTube.

"Yeah, it's been kinda slow, but I can see it picking up," Reka said. "It's a heavy traffic area, but there's a lot of competition around here, too.

"That ain't no major issue," Kev said. "Always remember, quality over quantity." He turned to E.

"You just make sure you let Reka handle all the transactions 'cause these niggas is real territorial around here, and if they get wind that it's you who opened up shop, they gon' close shop real quick."

"So what you want me to do?" E asked.

"Nothing really, just play the background and collect and protect the money, and make sure Reka's safe."

"I'mma need a strap," E said.

Kev pulled out a Ruger 9mm that was tucked at his waistband and held it out to E. E took the gun and looked it over like it was a new toy.

"You know how to use that?" Kev asked.

"It can't be that hard... cock it back, point and squeeze," E said, then extended his arm pointing the pistol at the door sideways. "Don't move, muthafucka," he said jokingly. "I'll blast your bitch ass."

Kev reached out and lowered E's arm then took the pistol back from him. "See, you playing, but this shit is serious business. First you always gotta check and see if your gun is even loaded," Kev said, then popped out the clip and showed E a fully loaded magazine, then slid it back in. "Then make sure the safety isn't on. Cock it back, then blast a bitch ass nigga." He handed the gun back to E with the safety on. "Tuck that shit man, we 'bout to get up out of here. Reka, we going to a party tonight. You gon' hold down the spot for me?"

"Which one?" she asked.

"Greenwood, that's the fa sho money," Kev said.

"Of course, baby, you know I got you."

Kev gave her the drugs. He didn't have to explain to her what he expected back in return because they already had an understanding.

Out of the $700 dollars' worth of crack Kev had just given her, she would bring him five-hundred dollars back. Kev didn't care whether Reka smoked or sold her share as long as his money was straight, and ever since they had started this system it always was.

"I'mma drive the Charger tonight, Reka," Kev said, deciding to drive the rental instead of his new car to the party. "I want you to drive my car home and park it behind the house."

He gave Reka his keys and got the keys to the Charger, then he and E left. They stopped at a local store which doubled as a liquor store and drive-thru convenience store.

"How you gonna buy a bottle from here?" E asked knowing that Kev looked exactly his age.

"Watch," Kev said, as he pulled the car into the drive-thru garage and up to the window where the Arab salesclerk was waiting. "Woeday, young Kev, what's up my nigga, I didn't know it was you. This you?" the Arab asked speaking of the Charger. "Na, it's a rental," Kev answered. "What's good though, you alright?"

"Yeah, everything's good, what can I do for you?"

"Let me get a fifth of 1738, 12-pack of Heineken, and a pack of Backwoods. You want something?" Kev asked, turning to his friend.

"Yeah, let me get a pack of Winterfresh," E told the attendant. The Arab rung up the items and passed them through the car window to Kev. Kev overpaid the man and told him to keep the change.

"Good looking Kev, you one hunnid," the Arab said, sounding, more like a Black man than an Arab. As Kev prepared to pull away, the Arab shouted out, stopping him.

"What's up?" Kev asked.

"You got any of that gas you be smoking for sale?"

"What you was tryna get?"

"Just a dub."

Kev pulled out an ounce and eyeballed a twenty out of the bag and gave it to the Arab in exchange for a twenty.

"That's gelato, it's smoking'," Kev said.

The Arab raised his hand to his nose, smelling his purchase.

"Whew. That's that pack right there, woeday, good looking out my nigga."

"No problem," Kev said, as he put the money away then drove off.

E and Kev rode around drinking and smoking, catching plays, and turning corners until it was time to go to the party. E didn't smoke but was hitting the Remy like a champ. When they finally pulled up, the street was crowded with cars and people. After finding a parking space and parking the car, Kev and E put their guns in the glove box and got out and walked toward the house. They knew they wouldn't be able to get in with their guns because of the person with the metal detector wand at the door. There had been so many shootings at house parties that it was now common practice to have a metal detector present and was even now welcomed by the guest. It didn't stop the shootings though, just made sure they happened outside.

Kev and E could hear the music coming from the house as they approached and could see a crowd of people gathered on the yard and front porch. Kev and E were probably the youngest out of all the high school kids that were present, but no one seemed to notice or care as they walked up. All the kids saw was that they had brought beer and liquor.

Kev and E took the alcohol in the house and put the beer in the kitchen, and that's when E saw Tiffany, the girl he'd met earlier that day. He motioned for her to come to him.

"Hey," she said over the music then gave E a hug. "I'm glad y'all came."

"Wouldn't have missed it for anything in the world, I been thinking about you all day," E said with a smile.

"Aww... really? You're so sweet, why don't we go downstairs where the real party is..." she said, then turned to Kev. "Erica down there and she been talking about you all day."

"Is that right?" Kev asked not the least bit surprised. He knew Erica would be all over him after the display he'd put on in his new whip.

"Yep, she likes you, but don't tell her I told you. Come on, follow me."

They made their way to the basement stairs and went down into the dark basement where the bulk of the party was. The only illumination came from two red light bulbs that seemed to only make the smoke visible.

Tiffany led them to a section off in the corner where there was a crowd of people sitting on a couch and in a few chairs. Kev instantly, recognized Erica sitting in the middle of the couch smoking a blunt with a guy sitting on each side of her. When she saw Kev standing in front of her with E and Tiffany, she passed one of the boys the blunt and jumped to her feet.

"Kev..." she said with a smile then gave him a hug, pressing her body against his in the process. "I was just thinking about you. Come and sit down," she said then grabbed his hand and led him over to the couch where she had just gotten up from.

"Let me get this couch y'all for me and my friends," she said to the remaining occupants of the sofa.

The guys stirred but was reluctant to get up and lose such a good seat, especially after letting her smoke their weed.

"C'mon, move, ya asses," she urged then grabbed one of the guys by the wrist and assisted him up.

"Damn, Erica, it's like that?" The guy whose wrist she'd grabbed said as he watched her sit next to Kev and Tiffany and E on the couch.

Erica looked at him a moment before answering as if contemplating her answer. "Yeah, I'mma holler at you later though, alright?" she said with a trace of resentment. The guy shook his head and walked off.

"Who was that?" Kev asked her once the guy was out of sight.

"That's just my friend Kemon."

"I think he likes you."

Erica smiled again. "Of course, he likes me, everybody do... but I like you," she said then got up and sat back down on his lap.

"Is that right?" Kev asked nonchalantly even though he was getting aroused.

"Mm-hmmm." She tried to kiss him on the lips, but he turned his head in time giving her his cheek, but still smelled the alcohol on her breath.

"You too good to let me kiss your lips?" she asked, showing the beginning stages of an attitude.

"Na, it ain't like that. It's just that I've been drinking and smoking, and my breath might not be right," Kev lied as he chewed on the stick of Winterfresh.

"Oh, you got some weed?"

"Yeah, I got a little... you know how to roll?" she nodded her head.

Kev handed her a Backwood with some weed in it and watched as she expertly rolled it up and lit it. He knew she was a real weed smoker because not everyone could roll a Backwoods right.

They passed the blunt around until it was gone, and Kev took note that Erica had not choked once.

One of the hottest female rappers came blasting through the speakers and both Tiffany and Erica jumped to their feet and started dancing. Erica grabbed ahold of Kev and led him into the crowd then turned away from him and grinded her ass on him to the beat.

"She a rich nigga bitch!" Every girl in the basement yelled at the same time along with the song.

They danced throughout the entire song and into the next one getting freakier with each other as the song progressed. Kev was starting to feel her. She moved her body to the beat like an expert, and she let his hands explore her body freely.

Before the second song ended Kev caught sight of a commotion by the couch where E was still sitting and saw a fight had broken out. He stopped dancing and focused on the figures tussling in the shadows.

"Shit, that's E," he said then darted towards the fracas.

E was standing tall, battling the same two guys who Erica had made get up from the couch. The boy named Kemon never saw Kev coming and Kev's punch caught him flush on the bridge of his nose. Kemon fell to the ground with both his hands held over his nose, while Kev helped E pummel the other guy. Right when the guy fell to the floor it seemed like the whole party rushed at Kev and E and attacked them.

Before he even knew what was going on, Kev found himself on the basement floor trying to cover himself from the kicks and punches that were raining down on him. All he knew for sure was that E was lying next to him undergoing the same thrashing.

The twenty seconds that he lay on the floor getting kicked felt like sixty minutes before they stopped and he heard Erica's voice yelling for the crowd to get back, followed by her hands closing around his shoulders.

"It's okay, Kev, it's me, come on, let's go." She helped him to his feet as Tiffany did the same for E. The two girls led them through the crowded but now silent basement as everyone watched.

When they made it upstairs, Kev was hurt but grew animated.

"Tell everybody the party over," he said to Erica.

"What? No... it's too early. It was just a little fight, Kev. C'mon to the back and let me make sure you're alright," she said, trying to entice him to her room.

"Look Erica, this party over. Either you get everybody out or I'm gonna shoot this bitch up wit everybody in it." He turned and walked away without saying another word and E followed behind him.

"Bitch ass nigga stole me," E said as they reached Kev's car.

Kev opened the passenger door then the glove box and passed E the Ruger then took out and cocked back his .380, putting a bullet in the chamber.

"What you tryna do, Kev?" E said with a serious look.

"Ain't nobody gon' put they hands on me like that and get away with it," Craig had always told Kev that if he let something like that slide once without doing anything, it was sure to happen again, and again, and only get worse.

"So, you wanna bust that dude Kemon?" E asked.

"Nope, I'm gonna bust all them niggas along with him too."

They started walking back to the party but stopped short of the house and just stood in the shadows and watched.

"When Kemon and that other nigga come out, we start shooting and don't stop 'til we empty the clips. Try to hit them and whoever else wit 'em."

E wanted to protest but his anger wouldn't let him. He cocked the slide on the Ruger back and watched and waited to see his prey.

It didn't take long before Kemon and his buddies exited the house and Kev held up one finger telling E to wait until they stepped fully off the porch so that they couldn't run back inside. To Kev's dismay, he saw that Erica was walking and talking with Kemon.

"That's your girl with him, ain't it?" "Man, see if she go back inside, if not..." Kev shrugged.

She kept coming. As soon as the last person of the group stepped off the porch, the first shots rang out.

POP! POP! POW! Hit in rapid succession. The shots came from both Kev and E's guns causing havoc and pandemonium.

The first three shots all found their targets before people started getting down, and scrambling for cover. After firing the initial shots, both Kev and E's adrenaline spiked and carried their shooting spree on. They didn't care who they hit now, they just licked off shots blindly into the crowd until both their guns were empty. They then turned and ran back to the car and drove off with tires squealing.

CHAPTER 7

Things were bad. Kev thought as he lay in the bed in his room next to Karma. Then he corrected himself. Things actually weren't really bad but it wasn't peaches and cream either. There wasn't any heat or beef over the house party shooting that had taken place a few months back, but what Kev was dealing with seemed worse than if that had gone sour. He was dealing with the everyday problems and nuances of life. Karma's stomach was showing her pregnancy. E didn't have a knack for the drug game, even with Reka's assistance, and his mom found a reason to kick him out of the house it seemed like every week.

"What's wrong, baby?" Karma asked after finishing sealing the blunt she'd been rolling.

Kev took a deep breath before answering. "Stressed, girl... just tired. It just seems like nothing ever goes as planned."

He accepted the lit blunt from Karma and took a toke, inhaling deeply then blowing out the smoke slowly.

"So what you gon' do about school?" he asked.

"I don't know Kev. I want to finish but I feel uncomfortable walking around pregnant. It feels like everybody is staring and talking about me."

"You can't drop out of school, Karma."

"Who said I was dropping out? I'm just gonna sit out the rest of this year. Next year, the baby will be here and I can go back."

"That's what everybody be saying and they never do."

"Well I am. Look, just forget it, you don't understand. Let me hit that blunt," she said, then reached out and plucked the blunt from his hand before he could protest.

"You don't need to be smoking either."

"I know, I'mma quit. I promise. It's just a lot going on right now," she said, with smoke coming out of her mouth.

A knocking came from the door causing Karma to cover her exposed breast with the bed sheet. Kev got up, put on some pants, then walked over to the door and opened it. It was Reka.

"Yo momma down there trippin' talking about you need to get yo own place and shit. I told her she was trippin."

Kev could hear his mother's voice coming from downstairs. "... think he just gon' lay up in here and make babies all day. Sorry mutherfucka got me fucked up. Him and that little hoe. I ain't watching no snotty-nosed rugrats either."

"Can't you break her off something to shut her up?" Kev asked.

"That's the problem, she already straight, she got a little money."

Kev made a face that said he should have known. Every time his mother got a little money and felt she didn't need him for anything, she would start the shenanigans.

"Come on Karma, put some clothes on."

"Where we going?"

"To get a room. Say Reka, I'mma leave you something to hold the house down wit, alright?"

"How long you gon' be gone?" Reka asked.

Karma rolled her eyes. Her and Reka's relationship hadn't gotten any better. Kev ignored Karma's attitude. "We'll probably be gone the whole weekend."

After packing a few things and giving Reka some work, Kev locked his bedroom door and left with Karma. He called E while he was in the car.

"What up, my nigga?" was how E answered the phone.

"Drama. Same ol' B.S. Look, my mom's tripping again so me and Karma 'bout to get a room at the Best West for the weekend."

"You know you can stay here, we got an extra room if y'all don't mind the mess," E said then laughed.

"Nah, we good. Karma ain't going for that."

"Alright then cuz, that's what's up. I should be getting at you soon about that paper too, if this move go through."

Kev doubted that it would go through, but didn't say so. "Alright, that's what's up. Just hit me up."

Kev ended the call as he was pulling into the Best Western parking lot. They checked into the hospitality suite at the rate of a regular room because Karma's friend worked as the Assistant Manager and also because they were such frequent visitors.

They didn't spend much time in the suite after checking in though because Kev's phone was ringing non-stop with customers.

"You see how good God is, baby? He never closes a door without opening a window. We gon' make a lot of money tonight, watch."

"Um, I hate to sound negative, but I don't think God has His hands on your drug empire."

"You see, that's where you're wrong at, babygirl. God got His hand in everything."

Karma didn't say anything else on the subject, choosing not to debate even though she disagreed entirely. To her, it was obvious that sometimes the devil was at work.

Finally, after running back and forth from the hilltop to the valley, going from house to house, catching plays, there was a break in the action and they pulled up to the trap house on Haynes where E was posted with the girl Tiffany from the house party him and Kev had shot up. Erica, the girl whose party it was, had come within inches of getting shot herself that night, along with the six others that had actually gotten hit. She wasn't mad though, or at least she claimed she wasn't and she even still tried to talk to Kev through her friend Tiffany with a message here and there, but Kev didn't trust her and wasn't feeling her anyway, he was all about Karma.

He and Karma sat on the front porch with E and Tiffany, in white plastic chairs. They sipped on drinks and passed a blunt back and forth while listening to music and talking. Kev allowed Karma to smoke weed, but he drew the line at alcohol, so she was the only one who wasn't drinking.

Kev and E talked business in a hushed tone, while the girls jabbered on about pregnancy and the upcoming baby shower.

"I don't understand how you not gon' be ready. You should be super straight by now," Kev said, while shaking his head.

"I mean, I got some paper, just not enough yet. I need a lil more time... a few more flips and I should be straight."

Kev was mad but did his best to hide it. He needed E to have that five grand in order to purchase the half of kilo Fred had waiting for him. He knew E had been blowing his money on clothes and girls, because he did the same. He also knew there wasn't much he could say or do about it because in the end, it was E's money. He just wished he would save more.

"Me and Karma about to get our own place," Kev changed the subject. "I'mma have Reka put it in her name. I hate to leave mom's house because it's such a gold mine, but she be tripping too much. It's every week now."

"You can't be mad Kev, you know what they say, mo' money, mo problems," E said, then raised his glass for a toast in which Kev participated, agreeing with him wholeheartedly. He could see the truth in that statement firsthand.

They finished off the bottle they were drinking and Kev decided it was time to go. Karma was tired and Kev had a play to catch before they would head in, so they said a few parting words and left.

Kev's head was spinning but he felt okay enough to drive. All in all, he was feeling better and his attitude was contagious because Karma was in a good mood, too. They cruised up East Avenue listening to Karma's Mariah Carey playlist while Karma tried her best to sing along with her even though her voice kept cracking and breaking up making Kev laugh.

"*When you left I lost a part of me, is that so hard to believe...*" Kev was smiling and looking at her, he didn't see the light turn red. "*... come back baby please!*"

BANG! The sound was horrible.

It was the sound of metal scraping and tearing through metal—a deep shrill, then the music stopped along with everything else.

Kev was unconscious and had no clue what had happened. Everything was darkness. The next day he woke up in a hospital with a doctor and a nurse standing over him. "What happened?" he asked, groggy from the morphine in his system.

The doctor spoke in a clear, curt voice, "You've been in an automobile accident and have suffered a concussion, a broken arm and a broken collar bone."

Kev hadn't felt any pain, but at the mention of his injuries, he immediately felt them throbbing and involuntarily let out a moan. At once he thought of Karma and the baby and almost leapt out of the hospital bed. "What about Karma? Where's Karma?"

The nurse and the doctor exchanged solemn looks that prepared Kev for the worst. The doctor shook his head, then spoke again. "She didn't make it Kevin, her or the baby."

The extent of Kev's pain emanated out of him and filled the whole room with its silence. He felt completely hollow inside, and was in such shock that the tears fell from his eyes without him even noticing.

The doctor's voice brought him out of his deep reverie. "Kevin, there's some police officers outside this room waiting to talk to you, do you feel up to it?"

He really didn't want to talk to the cops, but figured he didn't have a choice. He told the doctor it was okay then waited for his blue-blooded visitors to enter. As if things weren't bad enough, the police only made matters worse.

They told Kev that according to the witnesses, the accident was his fault because he had run a red light, and also that they had found a heavy amount of alcohol in his blood sample, and crack cocaine in the car. Then they told him that they were going to have to charge him with two counts of vehicular manslaughter for the death of Karma and the baby, the driver of the other car had suffered only minor injuries.

Kev was numb to the news, he didn't care and showed no reaction whatsoever to their dismay. All he could think about was the news the doctor had given him about Karma and the baby. He questioned if he were somehow cursed by some unknown source for some unknown reason. He promised himself that he'd never love anything again because all it seemed to bring was pain.

He was released from the hospital the next day directly into police custody. He sat quietly in the patrol car as if he were thinking, but he wasn't, he was just there, going with the flow. They took him to Dan Street where he was booked in the Juvenile Detention Center. With his first phone call, he called Reka and explained the situation to her, unable to hold back his emotions or his tears.

"It feels like my life is over," he cried into the phone.

Reka assured him that it wasn't and that things would be okay. She told him that she'd contact E and that the both of them would be at his bond hearing in the morning to do whatever it took to get him out. Kev thanked her then hung up the phone and was led by an officer to an open dormitory that was eerily similar to the one he had stayed in at the group home. He didn't speak to any of the other inmates as he made his way to his bunk and was thankful that none of them tried to speak to him either. He laid down on his bunk fully clothed and uncomfortable because of the cast on his arm along with the sling.

He knew sleeping was out of the question with the amount of pain he was suffering, along with his racing thoughts, so he just lay there and tried to visualize Karma; all the small details, from beauty marks to scars. After laying in the same position for hours, he was broken out of his trance by a Corrections Officer standing in the doorway screaming "chow call" at the top of his lungs. Kev jumped off his bunk a little startled at the vocal intrusion and joined the line at the door awaiting his tray.

When he got it, he looked at the lumpy oatmeal, processed sausage, and freezer burned waffle squares with disgust and refused to touch it. He offered the tray to the guy sitting next to him who eagerly accepted it, then went and laid back on his bunk and waited until they called him for court.

Court was held in the same building and Kev was appointed a lawyer in a cheap suit, which was disappointing because he looked dumb, but Kev's spirits lifted once he saw Reka and E already seated and waiting in the courtroom when he arrived. The judge was a middle-aged Black man who didn't hide his anger at Kev, and gave him a long speech about responsibility and consequences for his actions, but then softened considerably and told him that he understood he was suffering, also.

Kev breathed a sigh of relief when the judge issued him a signature bond. He looked back at Reka and E and let a smile show on his face, the first since being in the car with Karma. His happiness didn't last long though because the judge followed up his statement by adding that he could only be released to a legal guardian. Kev knew that the Johnsons were his previous legal guardians, and also that there was no way they'd come down here and get mixed up in this affair.

Thinking quick, now that his immediate freedom depended on it, Kev turned to his shabbily-dressed lawyer. "I need you to find Mr. Griggs for me."

"Who is that?"

"He was my counselor at the group home. He'll contact my legal guardians so I can get out of here."

The lawyer wrote down the address to the group home, then told Kev he'd take care of it. With his business in the courtroom being over, the bailiff appeared back by his side and proceeded to lead him out of the courtroom not allowing him to stop and speak with Reka or E. The bailiff escorted him all the way back to the dorm room where Kev would end up staying the whole time until he was sent to Indian River Youth Correctional Facility.

CHAPTER 8

Sometimes, Kev wondered why GOD had sent him here. Mr. Griggs had visited him, and they had sat down and read over the story of Job in the Bible and compared it to Kev's situation. Mr. Griggs was convinced that the message was clear, and that the moral of the story was that no one knows why God takes an action, but regardless of what that action may be, one should never question him and you should definitely never renounce him. The events in Kev's life made him skeptical, and he secretly did both question and renounce God. It seemed like everyone he had ever loved had been taken from him. Even Reka was M.I.A., and Kev guessed that she was probably bad off out in the streets strung out again. Even though their relationship had included sex, she was still the closest thing to a real mother he had ever known and he worried about her constantly.

In the year that he'd been locked up in Indian River, he had received exactly two letters from E. He received the first one while he was still on Dan Street, and all it was basically, was E asking Kev's advice on everything. E had no clue what to do now that he was on his own, and he knew it. The second and last letter Kev had received from him came a few months after the first and it basically stated that E was out there hurting and by himself. He did tell Kev that he still had the gun Kev had given him though, so at least he could rob before he'd starve. As bad as Kev wanted to help the both of them, the reality of the situation was that they were out there, and he was in here—a different world—one that provided him with enough problems of his own. When he had first arrived, he found himself constantly fighting. Kids would continually try him on petty stuff that Kev would actually rather just ignore and let slide instead of reacting and getting into trouble, but fighting was sort of like a rite of passage, and was the only way to get some respect and make the harassment stop. The first fight he was involved in went by quickly enough and left Kev with a bloody nose and sitting on his butt with a headache. The second fight went down differently. Kev was a quick learner and had learned to tuck his chin and let his hands fly freely. He didn't necessarily win that fight, but he didn't lose either, what he did do is gain some understanding that he would fight and wasn't a pushover and also that he actually hit pretty hard, too.

    The biggest kid in Kev's dorm was a kid named Carlos who was from Cleveland and was known for his good boxing skills. Everyone called him C. C was the only kid in the dorm who had been charged as an adult, and was only waiting on his eighteenth birthday to be shipped out to adult prison where he would continue his thirty-year sentence for robbery homicide.

    C respected Kev because Kev was a hustler who was on his own like himself. They were both children of circumstance and victims to similar fates. Their conversations were effortless and went along smoothly because neither one talked much which was a virtue they both appreciated.

At the moment, they were sitting on C's bunk playing their fourth game of chess that was coming down to the finish. They both had a queen, a rook and two pawns, but C had a bishop and Kev a knight—an even game. Kev kept putting C in check until C made a mistake and put his queen in jeopardy. Kev put him in check with a knight fork and took C's queen and eventually the game.

"You know where you messed up, right?" Kev asked.

C didn't answer, but instead only set the board back up.

Kev continued. "When I was checking you, you kept your king around your queen, trying to protect each other, but see, your queen can stand alone too, she don't need no protection. My bro used to tell me how much it was like life because you can't walk up on a queen and take her unless she comes to him."

At first, C thought Kev was just running his mouth, but then he thought of the wisdom of his words, and understood. They played a few more games before Kev had to go.

"I gotta go to class," Kev said, looking at the clock on the wall.

Carlos looked back at the clock too, checking the time. "Supersets when you get back," he said, talking about their workout regimen, which would include pull-ups, push-ups and dips.

"Yeah, I'm looking forward to it."

Kev wasn't being sarcastic; he'd loved the results he'd been seeing since he'd started working out. Not only could he see the difference, but he could feel it also. It felt good to him, he could literally feel the power.

A female guard entered the dorm and called for movement which was Kev's signal to head out to class. G.E.D.

class was taught by older inmates under the supervision of a teacher named, Mr. Krauss. Mr. Krauss was a middle-aged white man who could care less whether his students got their education or not. Just about all the work was done on computers and Kev couldn't stand any of it. He just figured it was all useless and in no way a test of true intelligence. He couldn't see how he would ever use algebra in his daily life or science either for that matter. He still did his work however and eventually received his General Equivalence Diploma, and although he tried to convince himself that it didn't mean anything, it made him feel good; it was an accomplishment. It was just sad that he had no one else to share his achievement with other than Mr. Griggs, who seemed genuinely happy and promised to help Kev land a job upon release.

The days, weeks, and months flew by in rapid succession with every day resembling the one before with only the slightest variation until the one day, Kev's whole world was shaken up once again.

E had written him another letter. Kev wondered what possibly E could have to say now as he walked back to his bunk with the letter in hand. The very first line of the letter let Kev know that it wouldn't be good news, because it stated plainly, "I've got bad news."

Kev continued reading and received the devastating news that his mother was dead; found strangled to death in their home. Now it was official, he was on his own completely.

CHAPTER 9

After the news of his mother's death, Kev fell into a state of depression that was hard to notice in his environment because it seemed that all the boys were going through similar phases. C had been shipped off to adult prison and Kev went through the day to day monotony of prison life alone as if he were an emotionless vessel. He rarely smiled and almost never laughed. Prison hadn't only taken his joy, but it seemed to be working on his soul too, turning it dark. His only solace came from his weekly visit from Mr. Griggs, who acted as his mentor, psychologist, and father figure. He had been instrumental in seeing to it that Kev's mother was cremated and given a proper funeral. The state had allowed Kev to attend the one-hour ceremony in which he, Mr. Griggs, a prison guard, and the reverend were the only people in attendance. Once it was over, Kev tried to play it off like it was just a waste of time, but in actuality, it felt good being able to say goodbye.

As he walked the hall on his way to the visitation room where Mr. Griggs was waiting, the other inmates walked past without speaking or acknowledging him in any way. People had been keeping their distance from him ever since his demeanor had changed, they rarely even made eye contact.

When he entered the visitation room, he immediately spotted Mr. Griggs sitting near the back of the room waiving at him beckoning for him to come and join him. Mr. Griggs was dressed casually, as always, wearing blue jeans, a t-shirt, along with some basic Nike tennis shoes. Kev respected that about him. Even though he was successful and had good money, he didn't waste it on frivolous things like clothes and shoes or jewelry.

"What's up, Kevin?" he said, as he rose to his feet to give Kev a hug.

"Same 'ol, same ol. Every day pretty much the same in here, you know."

"Well not today, because I got good news."

The haze lifted from over Kev's eyes and he showed interest. He hadn't had any good news in what seemed like his whole life. "What's up?"

Mr. Griggs smiled that infectious smile of his. "I got you a job."

That was good, Kev thought, but he didn't see how it would help him while he was in here. "That's what's up. You know I appreciate it, but it just don't do me no good while I'm still in here."

"That's the best part, you're getting out of here, too."

Kev heard what he said, but wasn't sure he understood. "You mean they're letting me go?"

"Yep. They're going to release you into my custody, but you will be on probation until you're 18. As long as you keep your nose clean and stay out of trouble... You can stay out of the juvie joint. How 'bout it? You think you can go three years without breaking the law?"

Kev thought that he could go three years without getting caught, but still answered yes.

"Good, it's a done deal then. All that's left is the paperwork then we gon' get you out of here. How that sound?"

Kev shook his head as if saying this was unbelievable. "Thanks, man... I don't know what I'd do without you."

Mr. Griggs smiled again. "You'd do a little more time."

Kev was released into Mr. Griggs's custody on a Friday. The very first thing he did after his release was have Mr. Griggs take him to his old home on Greenwood. It looked like a haunted house once again, but Kev wasn't scared like the night he had come here from the Johnsons. He had grown a lot since then. The doors were locked, but that wasn't even a small problem for him, because he knew of at least three different ways to get inside. While Mr. Griggs waited in the car, Kev made his way to the back of the house and slid open the kitchen window then climbed right through it.

Once inside, he made a beeline straight to his old room. When he saw the door open and splintered where the pad lock sat, he had a bad feeling in his stomach. Upon entering the room, the first thing his eyes landed on was the piece of baseboard laying on the floor exposing the hole in the wall that was his stash spot. His legs moved him towards it unconsciously, and when he reached the wall he was reluctant to drop to his knees and search for his money that he knew wouldn't be there. He went through the motions anyways and proved his intuitions correct. He had been robbed. He walked back to the car with his head held down thinking which one of the three might have done it: Reka, his mom, or E.

If it were Reka, he thought to himself, she would have smoked it up. Same with his mother and if it was E, he would have more than likely fucked it up, so either way it was gone. When he got back in the car, Mr. Griggs sensed something was wrong, but he said nothing and just started the car and drove home.

Kev started his job the following Monday. It was the middle of winter and cold as hell outside, and he was working at a hand car wash on Copley Road, freezing his butt off, for a salary that was barely over minimum wage. Luckily, a lot of dope boys came to that car wash in their customized whips and left generous tips if you did a good job, and sometimes even if you didn't. Kev made sure he cleaned their cars meticulously, and was always over courteous; complimenting them on their taste no matter how ridiculous he really thought their elaborate paint jobs were. One day, during his first month at the wash, business was slow and Kev was stamping his feet and rubbing his hands together by a portable heater, trying to stay warm when a black Chevrolet Tahoe on 26-inch floaters pulled into the building. Kev figured this would be a big tipper, so he immediately picked up his towel and walked to the driver's door to see what all they wanted done.

The Tahoe's windows were tinted pitch black and as Kev approached, the driver's window slowly and silently slid down in its track. When Kev saw who was inside, he was blown away. E was sitting behind the wheel.

"What up, my nigga?" E said nonchalantly.

Kev was excited at just seeing his buddy and spat out a series of questions. "What up nigga? What's been good? Whose truck you in?"

E smiled. "This my truck bro," he said, watching to see Kev's reaction, then continued. "Yeah cuz, I'm finally eating."

Kev surveyed the truck once again, glancing over its rims and chrome trimmings, then settling his eyes on E and taking notice of his jewelry and fresh clothes. He then thought of his stolen stash of money, but quickly dismissed the thought.

"I don't know what you into, but you need to cut me in."

"That's what I was just thinking—whether you was gon' wash this thang or jump in."

Kev looked to his left, then his right, then threw his towel down and walked around to the trucks' passenger door and climbed in. "Let's ride."

E passed Kev a tightly rolled blunt as they pulled away from the car wash.

"Gone and put some fire to it. That's that Zaza right there," E said of the blunt.

"Man, you know I can't smoke 'cause they gonna piss test me, and I can't believe you smoking now."

"Yeah man, started smoking when I started stressing. You haven't failed a test yet have you?"

Kev shook his head no.

"Everyone knows you're allowed to fail the first one, just tell 'em you smoked while you was in," E said, passing on a prison urban legend he'd heard somewhere.

The myth sounded true enough for Kev, who wasn't about to put up much of a fight anyway, because he wanted to smoke.

He grabbed the lighter out of the ashtray and sparked up, inhaling a huge cloud of potent marijuana smoke in the process.

The weed was strong. The smoke hit Kev's lungs and burned like lava causing him to choke. His body shook with convulsions as he did his best to suppress his cough in order to keep all the smoke in his lungs.

E laughed. "That shit strong, ain't it?"

Kev regained his composure then passed the blunt to E. "Hell yeah, that shit strong. What the hell is it?"

"It's some new strain, they call it 'thrax, short for anthrax."

Kev reached out and received the blunt back from E and was careful not to hit it as hard as he had the time before. "I can see why they call it that," he said as he blew out smoke. "Shit almost killed me."

They finished smoking the blunt without saying much else. They were listening to the music which played a song that followed the new drill music trend that had started in the Chi. The high that Kev was experiencing blended good with the bass of the music and the comfortable ride the Tahoe provided contrasted perfectly with the cold bleak day outside its doors.

"So, you gon' tell me what you into that's getting you paid?"

E gave him a mischievous grin in return. "You ever heard of foe-foe-N?"

Kev had no clue of what E was talking about.

"You mean like them rims they be riding in Texas?" He asked.

E burst out laughing. "Na man, it's some shit my cousin in Atlanta put me on to. It's got to do with checks and business accounts and shit. It's basically just bouncing checks and scheming on banks, but they call it foe-foe-N, and it makes real money, real quick."

Kev knew that bank fraud was a white-collar crime that paid well, but he also knew that it left a paper trail. "Don't that shit leave a paper trail?" he asked.

"Of course, but if neither the checks or accounts is in my name, then I'm the invisible man."

Kev saw his reasoning, and could see how it was true, but he also saw that X-factor which was that the person whose name the account was in would have a paper trail leading to them and they would know you, which made it possible to get set up.

E took notice of the doubt on Kev's face. "Don't worry, bro. It's foolproof. Look at me. I been doing it all year and you see I'm still out here. Just watch, fuck with me, and you about to see more money than you've ever seen before the weather change." That sounded good to Kev. So good that he didn't have to think any further about his decision. "I'm in, bro. Let's do it."

CHAPTER 10

Word on the street was that Kev's mom had been hanging out with a crackhead named Reggie prior to her murder. Kev cruised his old neighborhood in different rental cars almost every day in search of Reka in order to ask her about what had happened, and found her after only a couple weeks of searching. He saw her haggling a drug dealer for some work. Even from a distance, he could see that she looked bad. Her hair was disheveled, her clothes looked worn down, her shoes were dirty and she looked to have lost a lot of weight. Kev debated on whether or not to pull over or keep going, but he was only fooling himself because he knew he had to stop if for nothing else than to get some answers about his mother's murder.

"What's up, Reka?" He called out the window as he rolled up on her.

Reka stopped talking and looked to see who was in the car. When she saw it was Kevin, she let out a genuine scream of joy then rushed to the driver's door.

Kev stepped out of the car and let her embrace him even though she smelled a little rank.

She released her grip on him then stepped back and looked him over. She noticed that he had put on weight and was muscular. Even though he looked good, he didn't look like his old self though, which was always a teen in her eyes—he seemed more mature.

"When did you get out?" Reka asked.

"I been out about a few months now. Was working at the car wash on Copley, but quit that. I been bussing some different moves lately."

"That's good. It looks like you're doing good. Where you staying?"

"Me and E got an apartment in Barberton, but I got something in the works to get my own place. What about you, where you staying at?"

Reka broke their eye contact and looked down at her feet. "I'm just out here Kev... just here and there."

Kev felt bad for asking and naturally wanted to help her, but knew there wasn't much he could do to put a leash on her habit now that he wasn't dealing in her drug of choice any longer. He decided to change the subject.

"What happened to my mom?"

Reka grew instantly livelier. "It was that sorry ass nigga Reggie she was with, I swear it had to be him. He used to always jump on her for any little reason. I know it was him that killed her."

Kev listened intently. He didn't know Reggie, but Akron was so small he was sure he'd have no trouble finding him. He was just undecided on whether or not he really even wanted to find him. Even though Brenda was his mom, he kind of felt relieved that she was gone because his whole life she had played the role of oppressor. He was debating if avenging her death was worth it.

Reka saw his thoughts. "Don't go and do nothing that might get you into trouble Kev."

Kev knew she was right because even though he had shed a few initial tears for his mother's death, he didn't feel any anger or desire for revenge. But then again, he couldn't see himself just letting his mother's killer walk around willy-nilly.

"Yea, well, we'll see."

A heavy silence fell between them. Reka sensed that they had nothing else to really talk about but she didn't want to let him go without getting something from him.

"You think you can loan me a few dollars so I can grab up a few necessaries."

Kev didn't hesitate. He reached in his pants pocket and pulled out a wad of cash. He thumbed through the money, peeling off $200 and passed it to Reka. He knew there was a chance that she'd spend it all on rocks, but there was also the chance that she'd handle her business and purchase the things she needed, too.

Reka took the money and said thank you while looking down at her feet trying to keep Kev from noticing the tears in her eyes.

Kev placed his pointer finger under her chin and used his hand to wipe the tears from her face.

"Reka, let me know when you get tired of living like this, okay, and I'll do whatever I can to help alright?"

The floodgates opened again and the tears came again.

"Aight, Kev... I'll let you know." Kev got back in the car and drove off. He had other business to handle.

As bad as he wanted to take Reka with him and help her change her life, he knew he couldn't. It was her choice. He removed Reka from his mind and headed for the bank. He had to meet a lady there so they could withdraw some money. The scam was simple bank fraud from bouncing some checks, and Kev didn't really like it, however, it paid the bills and then some.

Not a day went by that he didn't entertain the idea of getting back in the dope game, but E kept telling him to stick with the foe-foe-N because it didn't really carry any time if you got caught, unless you did the scam for over five grand—then it was a serious felony.

The lady Kev was on his way to meet was named Carla, and he had already deposited a $3500 check into her account the day before and was now about to withdraw the money. They were going to split the cash three ways: the girl who gave them the check would get a grand, Kev would get a grand, and Carla would pocket $1500.

After talking to Carla and watching him walk into the bank, he waited in the car listening to a song by Mozzy called, "Unfortunately". He liked the West Coast rapper a lot, he was pretty much all he listened to lately. He felt a lot of pain and struggle in his music that reminded him of his life. E was always trying to get him to laugh or just crack a smile, but Kev almost never did anymore.

When he saw Carla coming out of the bank with a huge smile on her face though, he knew she had the money. She opened the car door and then got in.

"You were right, I got it with no problem." She pulled out an envelope with the banks' logo printed on it and handed the whole thing over to Kev, who quickly counted out fifteen hundred-dollar bills and then handed them over to Carla and watched as she put it away in her purse.

"Thanks Kev, you're a lifesaver."

She leant over the center console and placed a kiss on his cheek. He started the car as Carla got out and got in her own car preparing to drive home with her newfound small fortune. It was not much but when someone is in debt, or has bills that are due, $1500 can indeed be a lifesaver.

Before they parted ways though, Carla leaned out her car window and invited Kev back to her house to smoke a blunt, which Kev knew meant the possibility of sex too. She was a pretty girl, although a little older than what Kev was used to, but he had other business to handle so he had to respectfully decline, but promised her a raincheck which he truly intended to cash. At the moment though, he had two more young ladies to meet at the bank so they could make similar transactions. If the transactions went through and the checks cleared, it would bring Kev's total take for the day to three grand, which would be amazing for one day's work and also right on time because he needed it. Before he even made it to the bank though, he received a phone call that would drastically change things.

"Hello?" He answered even though he didn't recognize the number.

"You have a collect call from (pause) 'E' who is an inmate at the Summit County Jail."

CHAPTER 11

E's bond was set at ten percent of $50,000. Kev went to a bail bondsman and reluctantly put up the five grand with hopes that E would make good on his promise of reimbursing him, because it was pretty much all he had.

When E got out and only gave him $2500, Kev did his best to hide his anger.

"What you do with all that money you was raking up?" Kev asked as they sat on the couch in their apartment smoking a blunt.

E blew out a cloud of smoke. "Man, cuz... I blew that shit, ain't no other way to put it, that's why I was trying to bust that move."

The move he was speaking of was the one that had landed him in jail. He had been trying to jug a USAA account for $30,000 and it had turned out to be a setup from the jump and now he was facing Federal time.

"Damn, that shit tweaky, bro," Kev said, then hit the blunt.

"So what type of time you facing?"

Before E could answer, Tiffany came out from a backroom and answered for him, showing that she had been listening.

"My baby ain't about to do no time, we gon' beat this shit. Ain't that right?" she said as she took a seat on E's lap.

Tiffany was the girl from the house party who E had been kicking it with ever since. Kev didn't know it at the time, but Tiffany was the one who had introduced E to the client that had set him up. Her friend Erica, the one who had thrown the party had been jocking Kev, calling him every day since she had caught wind that he was making money again. Kev had already fucked her twice, but he wasn't trying to get into anything serious with her so he tried to always be cold to her but she seemed unfazed by the treatment.

E kissed Tiffany on her lips. "Nah, I ain't about to do no time, cuz, I can't leave my baby." He kissed her twice more.

Kev was reminded of something his brother Craig use to say all the time. "The number one reason a nigga turn snitch is because he didn't want to leave his girl for the next nigga to fuck." He decided right then and there to keep a closer eye on his boy E and to stop jugging with him, period.

"You picking Erica up today?" Tiffany asked Kev.

"Naw, I gotta go handle some business, try and make some of this money back," he said, obviously taking a shot at E. "I might swing by there later though. What about you, E? What you got lined up?"

"It's been slow bro. I ain't got nothing going on. I had all my chips invested in that USAA jug. I need to bust a move though, bad."

The energy in the air had changed. The topic of finances had everyone thinking. Kev was amazed how things had gone from sugar to shit so fast. One minute, they were raking in bands and spending freely, and now they were scrambling to make money again.

Kev was skeptical. He didn't believe E didn't have all the money to reimburse him. He figured E was probably holding tight since it was too hot for him to bust another move.

Kev already had his mind set on what he was going to do though. It was simple for him to decide; it was time to go back to the basics. He told E he had to run and left the apartment. After making his last move, he headed straight to Fred's house with all the money he had left. When he got there, it looked as if they were passing out free food—there were so many people milling around. Kev knew the pieces of chicken Fred and Mel were passing out weren't edible though. They were serving weight so there were no crackheads or junkies hanging around, only ballers, and Kev recognized a few of their fancy foreign cars parked at the curbside.

Kev made his way to the front porch walking past the guys who were obviously goons and muscle for the ballers who were inside. He knocked on the front door and Mel opened it, holding a Mac-II with the clip protruding out of the handle. It wasn't' the gun that held Kev's eyes though, it was Mel. The tattoos on her face and all over her petite scantily covered body exuded sex appeal. Standing there in the doorway with the gun in her hand, she looked like a 2020 version of Foxy Brown.

"What's up Kev, where you been?" she asked, as she stepped to the side letting him in.

Kev shook his head. "I been trying this white-collar hustle shit, but it's really not my thing, you know?"

"Well, you're in luck 'cause me and Fred got something new going on that's definitely your speed."

"New?" Kev thought. There wasn't much new going on in the drug game since crack hit in '83 or meth which hit around the same time. Everything else had pretty much been around so now he was intrigued.

Mel led Kev straight to the kitchen, which was crowded but surprisingly quiet. Fred was standing at the island in the center of the kitchen wearing a Versace shirt covered by a Versace apron that Kev thought was fresh as hell. He gave Kev a nod once he noticed him enter the room, then he continued his demonstration.

"Now, I'mma take these 252 grams of china white and add only 10 grams of fentanyl along with my special cut which is actually nothing special or different from the cut most of you guys use already," Fred explained, then continued to mix his ingredients in front of the silent room.

"Now we have 500 grams of product, right? And I know y'all thinking that it can't be any good because of the amount of cut I used." Here he started smiling, showing off his gold teeth as a few people shook their heads in agreement. "But that's where you'd be wrong. I'd be willing to bet that whatever this product is now, it's stronger than any one that y'all can produce."

The room stayed silent. As much as they believed that just wasn't possible, they knew Fred rarely ever lost a bet, and he always bet big, so no one took up the wager.

"How's that possible?" One of the spectators asked. Once again, the smile showed on Fred's face.

"This fentanyl is a magic drug and it's going to make a lot of us very rich. Now, it's strong as hell. So strong that 1 gram of it used as cut on 10 grams of heroin might still be strong enough to knock down ten men—so you gotta be careful how you use it 'cause it's deadly."

"That's that shit that killed Prince." A heavy-set dark-skinned man draped in gold stated.

"And Michael Jackson," another one said.

"I don't know if this is it or not," Fred said. "But I do know it's what I'm using from here on out."

Kev stood silent in the back of the kitchen while the guest shot a volley of questions at Fred who did his best to answer them all. He knew what fentanyl was. He had read about it in Time Magazine while he was in. It was another prescription drug pushed out in society to get people hooked on pharmaceuticals instead of the natural drug. Now it seemed like everybody was hooked on pharmaceuticals, whether it be lean, percs, xan, fentanyl, or even the medical marijuana. The doctors were the new plug. He continued watching as business was conducted and transactions were made. Fred and Mel made a killing. Once the crowd had dissipated, Fred finally addressed Kev. "Man, I ain't seen you in a while lil bro, where you been at?" he asked.

Kev didn't feel like giving him a recap of everything he had been going through, so he gave him the short version which summed it up. "I been riding this roller coaster they call life bro," he told him. "And I'm still on it, bro. Still hanging on."

Fred understood and felt what Kev was saying, because even if it didn't show, his life was a rollercoaster too.

"So, what, you back now?"

Kev pulled out the money he had brought with him.

"It ain't much, but what'll this get me in dog food?" Kev asked, talking about heroin.

Fred took the money and counted it in front of Kev. It was $3000 total.

"I'mma tell you what I'mma do for you, lil bro. I'mma serve you two and a half ounces of boy for the three G's but since you my lil nigga, I'mma throw some of this Feddy Wap to you on the strength," Fred said, speaking of the fentanyl. You saw the demonstration, right?" Kev nodded.

"So, take this and turn your two and a half into five ounces, then come see me once you off it. You'll be sitting on a whole brick in no time."

A whole brick of heroin, Kev thought. That sounded about right.

CHAPTER 12

Fentanyl, or Feddy Wap, which is what everyone in the hood called it, was indeed a magic drug. The profits Kev made in his first week of selling his product cut with it were huge. Not only could he stretch his dope to the limit for maximum profits, but the customers preferred the dope that was cut with the fentanyl over the regular heroin that was floating around the hood. They even asked for it by name because it was that much stronger. The only knock on the so-called magic drug was that people were dying, and they were dying in record numbers. It was getting so bad that the mayor had went public speaking on the crisis. The latest news was that now if someone overdosed off the laced heroin, the authorities would investigate and try to find the dealer who had sold it to them, then charge them with murder.

The dealers were reeling and cowering away from anything having to do with fentanyl, and Kev was no exception. He was starting to stress and worry after every sale, and even though he was now adding less and less of the fentanyl, he knew all it took was one overdose and it could be his ass, game over.

E had been inquiring about Kev's recent influx of money since he had moved out. He was trying to see what Kev was into, but Kev was vague with his answers not wanting to risk giving E any ammunition that would tempt him to turn rat in order to stay out of prison. Kev plain and simple didn't trust E anymore, not with that pending Fed case looming over his head, and that girl in his ear. E could feel Kev's distrust and it made him resent him. He thought they were supposed to be brothers, sort of like G-Money on "New Jack City".

The tension was so strong every time they were together that they both avoided those encounters as much as possible now and rarely saw each other or even talked.

Erica, however, was the exact opposite. Ever since Kev had started back selling drugs, she had become a fixture in his life. Surprisingly, Kev actually welcomed her company now. He knew she was superficial, but her presence alone had become therapeutic and helped him deal with being alone in this world especially since the loss of Karma was always in the back of his mind.

"Do you love me, Kevin?" Erica had asked him one day, while they were lying in bed after making love, listening to an R&B singer croon through the stereo.

Caught up in the moment, Kev had answered yes. When she replied that she loved him too, Kev doubted her sincerity, but went along with it which led to her moving into the apartment with him.

Moving Erica in wasn't' that bad though, as a matter of fact, it was a win-win situation for Kev since she had a good job down at the hospital, and she would cook, clean, and sex him up pretty good, too. The only bad thing was that he knew the love wasn't real, and she was nosey as hell, making sure she knew all of his business. He knew she was a common gold-digger, who went for the boys with the money and would be gone as soon as the money was, but that didn't matter. As of now she was lovingly right by his side, his "ride or die bitch", as she called herself.

They were currently at their apartment waiting for a customer and having a conversation about their involvement in dealing fentanyl.

"I don't get it," she said. "I mean, it's the person's decision to get high, right? So how are you responsible if they overdose?"

"I know, right? Then they act like we the ones making the shit. I don't even know what the fuck fentanyl is, better yet, how to make it. That shit come from a lab. Who the fuck Black own a motherfucking science lab besides Neil de Grasse Tyson?"

Erica started laughing. "Instead of Dexter's laboratory, you'd have Dante's or Deandre's."

They both laughed at her joke until they were interrupted by a knock at the door. Kev got up with his Glock 40 in hand and asked who it was that was knocking.

"Reggie." A voice answered from the other side in almost a whisper.

Reggie was the crackhead Reka had told Kev she suspected had killed his mother. Thanks to Kev's generosity, he was now one of Kev's customers hooked on fentanyl laced heroin, and Kev figured it was just a matter of time before he'd OD. If Kev wanted to speed up the process, it would be easy because all he'd have to do is serve him what they call a hot pack, which was a pack that was heavily laced with the fentanyl, which would guarantee death. He wasn't planning on doing it any time soon though because lately, Reggie had been one of Kev's main customers, spending big money, but the minute Reggie's money well dried up, Kev had a special pack with his name on it.

After serving Reggie, Kev left Erica in front of the TV playing the game console while he went to see Mr. Griggs.

Mr. Griggs had finally warmed back up towards Kev after months of not speaking to him. He had been mad at Kev for walking off the job he had gotten him, but even more so at the fact that he had made him look like a fool by deserting after he had been released into his custody. It wasn't the same as walking away from the Johnsons. Deserting him had made him a fugitive of the law and Mr. Griggs wanted nothing to do with that. Their relationship didn't resume until after Kev's 18th birthday, which abolished his sentence and fugitive status, so Mr. Griggs no longer felt guilty and like an accomplice.

Fifteen minutes after leaving his apartment, Kev parked his car behind a black Chrysler 200 in the driveway of a modest two-story brick home in the Kenmore neighborhood. It was a sunny summer day with a slight cool breeze and Mr. Griggs was outside working in his yard using a weed eater. He stopped and turned it off once Kev pulled into the driveway then waited for him to get out of the car before speaking.

"Kevin, what's good, my boy?" He took Kev's hand and patted him on the back.

"Tryna stay out the way man, and make a dollar out of fifteen cents."

"I heard that. As long as it's a legit dollar, it'll last. C'mon and take a load off."

Mr. Griggs led Kev to his backyard where they had a seat around a table on the back deck.

"Water?" Mr. Griggs offered.

Kev accepted the bottled water then twisted the cap off and took a swig.

"So, how's life been treating you, Kevin?"

"Good, I'm good," Kev answered honestly. "I can actually say that I'm happy at the moment. I got a roof over my head, gas in my car, money in my pocket, food in my fridge, and a pretty girl to share my bed with."

Mr. Griggs smiled at Kev's answer and lifted his water bottle which Kev met and bumped against his own.

"Sounds like you got it all figured out."

"Yeah, actually, I think I have. You see, America is run solely on capitalism, so it's simple, it's all about the money. If you ever have a problem or are looking for the cause of a problem, or the solution, just look for the money. It's that simple."

"You really believe it's that simple? Rich people have problems, too. Well what about dirty money? Is it just as good?"

"Donald Trump became President, hell, and Jay became a billionaire."

Mr. Griggs couldn't help but let out a chuckle at Kev's rationalization, he was still impressed by his insight. He understood his point, too. Both of these individuals had broken and bent countless rules to gain wealth and it had brought them success. He also understood what Kev was missing too though.

"What you say is true, but you're missing one point. The flipside to all that money and success is the problems that come with it that we don't see."

"I don't think they having too many problems," Kev said naively.

"Oh, they got problems, you're just not aware of them... and believe it or not Kev, you got 'em, too. We all do."

Kev tried to think of any real problems he had in his life and couldn't think of any. After going through all the pain and turmoil of his childhood, he really appreciated this rare period of peace in his life. "Well, I will say this... whatever problems I may have now, is nothing compared to the ones I've already overcome."

Mr. Griggs nodded his head and smiled. He liked that positive attitude. He believed that overcoming obstacles was a major part of life and success.

"I'mma keep it real with you, Kevin. You're doing well for yourself and I'm happy for you but I know you're not working. So I'mma tell you like this: if you're selling drugs, that's a big problem."

CHAPTER 13

Reggie's body was found in his room by the boarding house manager with the needle still stuck in his arm. Funny thing about it was that Kev didn't even sell him a hot pack, but the police still ended up seeking Kev for questioning.

They showed up at his apartment the same day they had found Reggie's body. Two male detectives, one Black and one White. The Black detective reminded Kev of Shaft, and the White one reminded him of John Travolta. Kev took it as a good sign that they didn't ask him to come down to the station though and instead just asked to step inside his apartment.

There wasn't any paraphernalia left lying around, so Kev welcomed them in and offered them seats which they both declined.

"Do you know Reggie Wilson?" The Black detective asked.

"Who Reg? Yeah, I know Reggie. He was just over here yesterday. What about him?"

"What was his reason for stopping by?" the white cop asked, ignoring Kev's question.

Kev knew that this would be a critical answer. He didn't know what all they knew, but he knew that if he got caught lying it would make him look guilty, but at the same time, he couldn't just tell the cops, "I'm dealing heroin," even if they did already know.

"He stopped by on business," Kev answered honestly enough.

"Aight, let's skip the bullshit because we don't have time for it," the John Travolta look-alike said. "We know what type of business you run," he lied… "And we know you're most likely the one who sold Reggie that death pack, but see that's not what we're here for."

"It's not?" Kev asked, a little confused now.

"Nah, we could care less about Reggie OD'ing," the white cop answered.

"Yeah, fuck Reggie, one less deadbeat junkie," the Shaft look-alike added.

"See Kevin, this isn't an investigation, it's a warning of what's about to happen," Travolta continued. "See, your boy Reggie? He's nothing."

"A piece of shit," added Shaft.

Then Travolta again—"but when this fentanyl shit starts hitting suburbia, and starts killing kids and good families, that's when it's going to be a big problem."

Basically, White America, Kev thought.

Now it was Shaft's turn to take the lead. "When that happens, we gotta start cracking heads," he said. "And in order to get to the top, we gotta start at the bottom. You got any idea who's at the bottom, Kev?"

Kev remained silent now.

"That's right, so if you aren't ready to do some real, hard time, or give up some names, now's a good time to get out the game," Shaft finished up. Warning delivered.

The two detectives left Kev's apartment laughing and smiling, talking about doughnuts and lattes. As soon as they were gone, Erica, who had been in the bedroom silently listening to the conversation, emerged with a scared look on her face.

"I thought they were going to arrest you," She said.

"Nah, they can't prove I sold him anything, shit, a dead man don't talk, but they dead-ass serious about what they'll do if a kid or some affluent white folks start OD'ing and I ain't even about to go out like that. Not at all."

"So what are you gonna do?"

"Hang that shit up for a while," Kev said, shaking his head. "I ain't never been no fool. I'm hot right now, so I gotta close up shop. I'll probably hustle some weed and work a job 'till this whole thing blows over. Shit, I was getting tired of it anyway."

Kev did what he said he would and stopped selling heroin, and started selling weed, and things changed drastically after that.

His cash flow slowed down substantially, and finding a job proved to be a lot more difficult than he had planned. All of a sudden, Erica was the breadwinner and the changes that came over her with that scenario were anything but subtle. She became stronger in the relationship and her attitude changed for the worse. She seemed to always have a negative air about herself and was always quick to argue, never biting her tongue, and letting her words cut like swords.

Kev's role had changed also, and with it so had his character. He had fallen deeply in love with Erica, and was more and more dependent on her as his weed business struggled mainly because they smoked most of it. He couldn't recognize it but he was living in a state of depression. Their lives were a seesaw that Kev saw no way of getting off of.

Erica became unbearable once Kev's cash flow basically dried up and the bills started piling up. She would spend more time on her phone talking, texting, and on social media, than she would talk to him.

Kev believed she was cheating but couldn't prove it. He constantly told her that if she wanted to leave him and be with someone else that he understood, but she'd refuse and they'd go on arguing. He loved her and wanted her to stay, but he was getting tired of all the fighting and verbal abuse that came with it, it was going on everyday and had him ready to strangle her.

One day when he was picking her up from work, he watched as she walked out of the hospital along with a young Black doctor. Kev sat in the car and stared at his live-in girlfriend, who he couldn't even have a decent conversation with anymore, looking this doctor in the eyes while hanging on to his every word and laughing at anything he said that probably wasn't even remotely funny. When Kev saw her lean into him his heartbeat quickened from jealousy, then felt as if it had fallen into a dark pit. When she got in the car without speaking to him, Kev was at a loss for words. He sat there for a full minute just looking at her and thinking of a way out. Now more than ever, he wanted to leave her but he was stuck; he had no money and nowhere to go. After the minute had gone by without the slightest bit of recognition from Erica, Kev started the car and pulled off without a single word exchanged between the two of them.

When they arrived at their apartment, Erica got out the car before Kev could even kill the engine. Kev was mad. At first, he had been hurt seeing the attention she was giving the doctor, but now, after how she had treated him, he was just angry. Instead of going into the apartment behind her, he started the car and drove away. He had no idea where he was going, so he just drove through the city contemplating his fate.

As he rode down Thornton Street, he saw a pretty girl in a mini-skirt walking alone, hips swinging from side-to-side. He pulled the car over to the curb and rolled down the passenger's window. The girl stopped walking and looked to see who was in the car.

"What's up?" Kev said.

Instead of answering, the girl opened the passenger door and climbed in before Kev could protest.

"Hey handsome, you looking for a date?"

Kev realized she was selling pussy. He started to protest but changed his mind because the prostitute was young and attractive enough with makeup on. "How much is it gonna cost me?"

"Fifty to fuck or thirty for some head," she answered flatly without a trace of shame.

Kev had exactly $37.00 to his name. He handed the girl thirty then pulled into the parking lot of an empty baseball field and let her go to work. It was getting dark outside and he wasn't worried about getting noticed, so he let his seat back and relaxed. She was both good and efficient at it, keeping a slow and steady pace, never breaking rhythm or stopping until the job was completed.

Kev offered to take her wherever she wanted, but she refused and instead said thanks and got out and started back walking that same walk that had enticed Kev. Kev's thank you went unheard.

Kev wasn't mad anymore and when he made it home he didn't want to do anything but shower and watch TV—Erica and her B.S. wasn't even on his mind anymore. When he walked in the apartment, she didn't ask where he'd been, and he didn't ask her about the doctor. The two of them just stayed in separate rooms watching TV until about midnight, which is when Kev decided to go to bed.

The bedroom was pitch black, and Kev slowly navigated his way to his bedside night stand searching for the lamp. His hand found a coffee mug instead, knocking it over and spilling cold coffee and disturbing Erica who awoke cursing.

"What the fuck?!" She said as she cut the lamp on that stood on her side of the bed.

"Damn, my bad, I ain't see it."

"Damn, a bitch can't even get no sleep around here. You know I gotta get up and go to work in the morning. Unlike you, I can't just lay around all day and do nothing."

"I said my bad..." Kev said trying to end the argument that was brewing.

"Humph, yo bad. You clumsy and sorry as hell."

That struck a nerve, which is exactly what she intended.

"Fuck you, bitch."

"Naw, you can't nigga, 'cause I won't let yo ass."

"I don't give a fuck about yo stank ass worn out whore pussy," Kev said, getting madder and madder. "Keep fucking who you fucking."

Erica smiled. "I will."

Before Erica could let her chuckle accompany her smile, Kev slapped her in the face. She was on him in an instant, like a cat. Kev had never hit her before, but she had been waiting for him to slip up and do it just so she could call the police and have his ass thrown in jail.

Kev tried to hold her off, but she was swinging and kicking wildly while screaming help at the top of her lungs trying to get the neighbors to call the cops. While he tried to hold her off and calm her down, she took her nails and raked them down his face drawing blood.

Kev balled up his fist and punched her in the face. She kept fighting and scratching, so he punched her again, then again and again until the blood started flowing and she loosened her grip.

He then placed both his hands around her neck and started squeezing. All the stress and pain of the last few months turned into strength that funneled into his hands. Erica's eyes were bulging and bloodshot, and her tongue protruded out her mouth and her face was turning blue. Her body went limp while Kev's hands were still around her throat.

His hands slackened their grip and he finally took notice of the situation.

Erica's face was a bloody mess, and her eyes were both swollen and had rolled up into the back of her head. She was still breathing but Kev didn't notice, he thought she was dead and now he was scared. He grabbed his gun and car keys, then broke for his car. He had no idea where he was going, all he could think of was "drive." He was sure that the police would be looking for him so he couldn't go to Mr. Griggs's place because he would never bring trouble to his home, so that was out of the question. He couldn't go to E's because they hadn't been talking for months now and their relationship was through. Besides, Tiffany wouldn't hesitate to try and find out what was going on. While these thoughts raced through his mind his foot grew heavier and heavier on the gas pedal without him even noticing. It wasn't until he saw the blue and red lights that he realized that he was speeding. The hairs on his arms stood up and he started sweating as he pulled the car over to the curb. He didn't know whether the cop blue-lighted him because of his speeding or because of the situation that had occurred at the house between him and Erica.

Officer Keller was a good cop. He hadn't been on the force for five years yet and people were already saying he'd make a great detective one day. He looked like a cop, and his wife looked like a cop's wife and even his three boys looked like they're a cop's kids. They all were white with brown eyes and sandy brown hair. Officer Keller was actually finishing up his shift when he saw Kev's car speed past. Without a moment's hesitation, he fell in behind Kev and blue lighted him.

After pulling over, Kev looked in the driver's side mirror and saw the cop get out of the cop car and start approaching, and Kev's heart froze. His fear was instantly replaced with hate and anger.

There was no mistaking that face, no matter how many years may have passed. It was the face that haunted his nightmares, the face that had changed his life forever. The face of the cop who had killed his brother in front of him. Instinctively, Kev grabbed his gun.

When the cop leaned his face down to Kev's window and opened his mouth to say his spiel, Kev shot him right in it; bullseye.

The bullet hit officer Keller in the mouth, went through his teeth and out the back of his head, lifting him off his feet and killing him instantly. Kev's tires were spinning before the cop's body hit the ground. His adrenaline was pumping but he didn't feel any fear, he felt good. Like he was cleansed and finally liberated. He screamed a guttural supernatural cry of anguish and triumph and felt a chill run from his legs to his spine. That feeling was only temporary though, and in no time the gravity of the situation weighed in on him and he grew more scared than he had ever been in life. Unconsciously, he drove to his old house on Greenwood that he had once shared with his mother and two brothers, who were all gone now.

Officer Keller was not the cop who had killed Craig. He knew the cop who had, and didn't like him because he made the shield look bad. When Kev had laid eyes on him, he was suffering from a delusional disorder caused by his mental breakdown. As a result, a perfectly good officer wouldn't make it home to his family and all the police brutality and unlawful shootings by the police on Black Americans would once again seem justified in some cop's eyes.

Kev's old house was boarded up, but Kev managed to enter it through the back door, which was already pried open. It was dark inside and Kev could actually hear the critters scurrying around throughout. He found a corner and took a seat on the floor, then placed his head in his hands and cried.

He cried a silent cry full of all the pain and despair he had ever experienced. He relived all the losses, all the struggles. Years of depressing memories raced through his mind in seconds. It was agonizing. He figured his life was over, and that he really didn't have any reason to live—not one. He never meant to hurt Erica, but she had intentionally provoked him and he had bit the bait, and now the cops would kill him. When that thought came to mind, he shook his head no. He wouldn't allow it. Without a second thought, he raised his gun to his temple and pulled the trigger, welcoming the darkness that followed.

The end.

EPILOGUE

Reka had the trick drop her off on Roselyn, which was the street right behind the street she was staying on. Guys could be creeps, and they treated crack whores as less than human, which is why she wouldn't let any tricks know where she lived. Rapes were common in this game, and never reported. She had procured three rocks of her own that would last her through the night and into the morning. So now, she was quickly headed home to get high, cutting through the houses, emerging into the backyard of her house.

Home to her was Brenda's old house, which was now boarded up, rat infested, and probably waiting to be torn down. She wanted better but her condition just wouldn't allow it, it had a hold on her and controlled her life. As she approached the house, she thought about what it would take to make her quit, and for good this time. "An act of God," she said out loud and laughed to herself.

"BANG!"

The gunshot penetrated the silence of the night and seemed to follow Reka's words like an exclamation point. There was no doubt in her mind that it had come from inside of the house. Any other time she would have heard a gunshot from that close, she would have turned and ran in the opposite direction as fast as she could, but her intuition pulled her towards it without giving it a second thought.

It was pitch black inside as always so she couldn't see anything.

"Anyone here? I know you're in here," she said in a low, shaky voice.

She refused to take another step until she was acknowledged. Two full minutes passed with her standing stock still before she heard something coming from the opposite corner of the room of where her makeshift palette lay. A low groan.

Still not knowing what was pulling her, she made her way towards the sound. After four steps in that direction, she kicked a metal object making it slide across the floor. She knew it was a gun. Her heart started pounding in her chest.

"Kev?" she said, because it just felt right.

Nothing. And then yes, there it was again. Unmistakably a low groan.

Reka went down on her hands and knees feeling along the floor as she crawled. Her right hand landed in the blood first and she knew it was blood and started crying. She reached out and felt the body.

She knew it was Kev. No question.

She checked for and found a pulse, then pulled out her "Obama phone" that she never used, and dialed 9-1-1.

After telling the dispatcher what was wrong and giving her the address, she grabbed ahold of Kev's hand. "You're gonna make it."

AUTHOR BIO

Will Brown is an American author born and raised in Akron Ohio. Throughout childhood, the author excelled at scholastics despite a rough upbringing in an impoverished neighborhood known for drugs and violence. Despite all the good people in his life and the guidance he received, the author's choice to succumb to his surrounding environment and be active in the streets eventually led him to a three-year prison sentence in the Federal Penitentiary's notorious Big Sandy USP at the age of 22. Once released from prison, the author moved to Atlanta, GA, started a family, led the life of an average working man, and was content. In 2008, the United States went into a recession turning the author's life along with other Americans lives upside down and into a state of turmoil not sure of how their bills would be paid or where their next meal would come from. Subsequently, the author once again found himself turning to crime which led to a 10-year prison sentence in the Georgia State Prison system. This time inside, the author used his time wisely and strengthened his mind, body, and soul through reading, exercise, and religious studies. He discovered classic literature and fell in love with the genre and tried to read as many books as possible which eventually led him to start writing himself. He was released from prison in 2020 and founded Literati Publishing Co. that same year, and he has hopes of one day making it the number one publishing company in the world.

In loving memory of:

My grandmother Clara and grandfather Charles, uncle Jerry, aunt Ruth, aunt Chunky, uncle Mane, aunt Betty, aunt Charlene, aunt Rachel, cousin Sammy Colvin, cousin Nita, cousin Donta Reynolds, cousin Kiddo, cousin Skylar, cousin Ernie, cousin Lawrence, Marcus Primes, Acea, Boo aka "choose", Amp Trav, D-dog and Darnessa, Pepper, Marquise Welch, Bashard, Spank, D BO, Big Coop, Mook Geez, Main Main, Dee Da Gee, Big Keon, Lil Lonnie, Lashay, Solo, Fonzo, Wayne Wayne, Bossman, Big Justice, Dontez Burns, Ak Ron, Twan Bethune, Twan Robinson, Micheal Johnson (L.A.) and all else who left us too soon.

Upcoming release: Coming winter 2021
MIDWEST MAFIA.
Contact for promotional deals.

Printed in Dunstable, United Kingdom

73725661R00070